MURDER IN
BLACK AND WHITE

MURDER IN BLACK AND WHITE

by

Evelyn Elder

RAMBLE HOUSE

Murder in Black and White ©1931 by Evelyn Elder

Drawings by Austin Blomfield, A.R.T.B.A.

ISBN 13: 978-1-60543-161-1

ISBN 10: 1-60543-161-3

Ramble House Edition: 2009
Cover Art: Gavin L. O'Keefe
Preparation: Fender Tucker

MY BEST THANKS ARE DUE:

TO A. B. H., SINCE HE INTRODUCED ME TO THE GAME OF TENNIS, AND FOR MUCH BE-SIDES;

To RALPH STRAUS, SINCE TO HIM AND TO A VAGARY OF MY MEMORY I OWE AN IMPOR-TANT FEATURE OF THIS NOVEL;

To AUSTIN BLOMFIELD, FOR HIS INVALUABLE AID.

E.E.

AUTHOR'S NOTE

When the reader has reached the end of Part Three he is in possession of all the facts needed to reach the solution of the problem. Such further facts as are introduced in Part Four (and they are virtually only two in number) are no more than confirmation of the theory which emerges from the rest of the book.

PART ONE

THE ARTIST RETURNS
FROM ABROAD

CHAPTER I

THE ARTIST RETURNS FROM ABROAD

A COCKTAIL PARTY was in progress at Henry Evelyn's studio. It should be made clear at once that there was nothing ordinary about it. The host, Henry Evelyn, for example, was in theory an architect and that evidently justified his possession of a studio; but he was an architect only for the reason which used to drive some younger men to Parliament, others to the Bar and others again to the Guards. In other words, it seemed proper to him to acquire a nominal profession; there is no record of any edifice built to his design except his own residence.

Then the studio. It was admirably proportioned, large and cool, and it boasted the conventional "north light"; but otherwise it differed very little from a large living-room, eminently suitable for the hospitality which a well-to-do bachelor may choose to offer to a varied acquaintance. It occupied the main part of the ground floor, the rest consisting of hall, stairs and kitchen; the two floors above it provided not only a sufficiency of bedrooms for Evelyn and his domestic staff (an efficient married couple), but also a smaller and more homely sitting-room.

It was noticeably modern, alike in its furniture, its lighting and its decoration, yet it was saved from the effect of restlessness which a surfeit of steel tubes is liable to produce by the view, afforded by the two tall French windows on its southern side, of a delightful paved garden. The garden, indeed, in its formal imitation of artificiality, and its blaze of colour liberated by Nature from the canons of angularity, was in striking contrast with the studio.

If the studio and its owner, whose elegant spick and span appearance in no way suggested either the painter or the working architect, were far from the conventional types, so too was the cocktail party. It was small; it was not one of those affairs where you stand back to back and shoulder to shoulder. It was not necessary for you to shout, and risk so complete an acquisition of the shouting habit as to become a startling figure at a staid dinner after the party. The guests all knew one another, and had no need to

grope conversationally in search of one another's interests or oc-
cupations. And finally, the cocktails were good—and well and
truly iced.

The quiet conversation of the eight or ten people in the room,
over which laughter rippled gently like a light breeze over a field
of wheat, was momentarily interrupted by the entry of Siddons, the
inferior half of the "married couple." He approached his master
(no other term could do justice to the dignity of his demeanour)
and murmured discreetly.

"Mr. Horder!" the latter exclaimed. "Splendid. Of course I'll
speak to him. Sam Horder, just back," he added by way of general
explanation. "I'll get him to come round at once."

And he hurried to the hall, followed by Siddons.

"Where has the infant Samuel been?" asked one of the men. "I
suppose *you* know, don't you, Phoebe?"

Phoebe Carstairs shrugged her slim shoulders.

"I'm afraid Sam gave me up as a bad job—oh, months ago,"
she answered, with an easy laugh. "He was never sure whether he
wanted to marry me or employ me, free of charge, as a model.
And I didn't want either."

"Poor Sam," Vi Halliday observed. "I do really believe he
could be an artist if he spent less time and energy in displaying the
artistic temperament."

"Don't you believe it." The speaker was a solid, sunburnt man
in the early forties, whose dark bushy eyebrows and moustache
seemed to suit his rather sardonic tone. "You can't be an artist if
you've money enough not to take your work seriously."

"What about you, Richard? Or isn't a writer an artist?"

"I? Good heavens. I depend on my pen for my livelihood. And
the more I earn, the worse I write."

"And the more you sell."

"Doubtless."

"How very inconsistent you are," said Tom Halliday.

"Certainly. What else is a cocktail party for?" the writer admitted idly.

"Now he's started to be clever," observed the first inquirer after
Samuel Horder's affairs. "When Richard Dawson starts to be
clever, I always know it's time for me to go."

Henry Evelyn had re-entered the room and overheard the last
remark.

"Don't be misled," he said. "George Appleton trades upon his
egregious athleticism to make people believe he has no intellect."

"I'm no more of a fraud than you are, Henry, pretending you're the kind of architect who knows nothing about architecture when all the time—"

"Rot," the writer interrupted. "Henry's the complete—"

"Amateur," Vi Halliday suggested.

"*Poseur.*"

"*Flaneur.*" This was contributed by Mrs. Beecham, and was accompanied by a smirk of superior knowledge. Her chief claim to distinction was the nickname of "Jam," which in fact was misleading, for people as a rule were readier to swallow her husband than her.

"At all events we all agree he shows a tendency to err," said Appleton, and was met by a chorus of expostulation.

"And what about Sam Horder?" Phoebe Carstairs brought the conversation back to its earlier topic.

"He's just got back from Paris, by the 5.30 boat train, I suppose. Apparently yearns for human companionship. So he's coming round here at once."

"Oh, good," said Mrs. Beecham, who liked to pretend that good-looking and eligible young men naturally enjoyed her society. She glanced a little maliciously at Phoebe Carstairs, who paid no attention whatever. Henry Evelyn coughed in mock embarrassment.

"I rather gathered that he did not yearn for the companionship of crowds: rather of the individual."

"Don't say it's Phoebe still." This from George Appleton.

"No, I don't. If you really want to know—our Sam seems to have got into trouble—"

His guests groaned.

"Not necessarily that sort," went on Evelyn. "In fact, I rather gathered it was something—well, more serious. And what he wants to do is to confide in a real man of the world—one who has knocked about a bit—"

"Capital description of an amateur architect," Dawson commented, with a characteristic twitch of his bushy eyebrows.

"Oh, of course, if we're not wanted—" Mrs. Halliday began in spurious indignation.

"Where's Samuel been to, then?" Appleton asked.

"Place called—let's see, St. Andre, I think."

"You don't mean the place where there's a tennis-court?"

"How too utterly strange," Mrs. Beecham said sarcastically. "I suppose that's a very rare thing to find anywhere but at Wimbledon nowadays?"

"Tennis," said Appleton wearily, "is not the same as lawn-tennis."

"Real tennis, he means," two or three voices broke out, with an undercurrent of anxiety; Mrs. Beecham failed to observe it, or the glances of reproof which were cast in her direction.

"Never heard of it," she said, with self-satisfied composure.

"That's torn it," Henry Evelyn murmured, not too gently for Appleton to hear: as, of course, he was meant to. That determined games-player proceeded, undeterred by the general expostulation, to embark upon a lecture on the merits of the best of ball games.

"Don't you believe him, Mrs. Beecham," Tom Halliday said. "It's a ghastly game. I watched George playing it once; in fact, I played in a four-handed game with him—"

"The single's the real game, you know—"

"I dare say. All I can say is that I found it infernally hard to hit the ball, and when I did it was usually to be cursed by George for not letting it bounce and make chase better than twenty or something; and we were for ever changing sides with our opponents for no reason that I could discover; and finally when it was all over I hadn't the foggiest idea who had won."

"And the man who plays that game pretends he's lacking in intellect," was Dawson's comment.

Appleton laughed good-humouredly.

"You must just take my word for it, Mrs. Beecham. It's a game in a million—though I admit it's not easy."

"Is it necessary to go to St. André to play it?"

He laughed again.

"Oh, there are quite a lot of courts. But they vary a bit, and one is always interested in the ones one doesn't know. The one at St. André is quite famous. And whatever young Horder may want in the way of company, I for one intend to stay and cross-examine him about it."

"As I think I hear his taxi, you'll all have to listen to the cross-examination," Henry Evelyn observed, smiling, though a certain gravity was discernible beneath his good humour.

"Not that, please," said Phoebe Carstairs. "Dearly as I love both George and Samuel, I can't bear that. I'll just kiss the prodigal in a motherly way, swallow another cocktail and move on to places where I'm more welcome."

The door opened: Siddons gravely announced, "Mr. Horder."

His welcome if affectedly boisterous was unaffectedly sincere.

"Sorry, Sam," said Evelyn, when the noise subsided. "I gave 'em a broad hint you'd prefer my room to their company, but—well, you can see for yourself."

"Couldn't bear to miss you," Phoebe Carstairs assured him with a languishing look. Sam Horder coloured and stammered and glanced away, and Miss Carstairs bestowed a broad wink on the rest of the company.

"Jilted!" she exclaimed, tragically.

Sam Horder was a presentable young man, slightly callow; some would have called him good-looking, others might say that he might become so. His ingenuous expression recalled that so frequently portrayed in advertisements—whether of raincoats, cigarettes or tennis racquets—but he could hardly claim to possess the same superhuman handsomeness. He was fair-haired and blue-eyed, but his cheeks were rather too chubby and his ambition to keep his head as sleek as a new pin was one which he could never achieve. His attire was hardly more of an artist's than his host's was an architect's: still, he wore a rather voluminous tie as his ensign of artistry, and in his private opinion a distinctly dashing one. Under his arm, moreover, he carried a portfolio.

"Pretty pictures?" inquired Mrs. Beecham, displaying her usual flair for the obvious.

"Er—yes, Jammie."

"Show!"

"Well—of course, one day—but—"

"Ah, the *Quartier Latin* still exists, does it?" Dawson suggested.

"Worse than that, I'm afraid," said Phoebe Carstairs. "It's—" and she whispered to Tom Halliday, who nodded solemnly.

"I'm afraid so. It *is* that sort of scrape," he informed his wife.

"Oh, Samuel! Who is she?" Vi demanded. "You might have sent us a snapshot."

"I say, do shut up," Horder protested, his cheeks now a deep red.

"Give him a cocktail first," Mrs. Beecham said; the others were clamouring for him to "tell them the worst."

"Well, if you must know, I did meet a jolly nice girl—"

"This! To me!" Miss Carstairs moaned.

"*Avec mes sabots,*" said Dawson.

"How d'you mean?" Apple ton promptly asked the writer, assuming his air of bovine stupidity.

"Is she really French?" Tom Halliday asked. "Because if so you can't have got very far. You should just hear his accent."

"Man of deeds," Dawson answered.

"As a matter of fact, she's English," Sam Horder said, rather annoyed by all this chaff. "And I'd met her before—or practically."

"The suspense is awful. Who *is* she?"

"No one you'd know, Phoebe."

"Oh, Sam! Don't say she's 'that sort of a girl.' What will your uncle say, the rural dean, I mean?"

"Why don't rural deans wear gaiters? I think it's a shame," Mrs. Beecham put in, but no one took any notice of her—properly enough.

"Obviously a clergyman's daughter," Vi Halliday commented.

"She's a very nice girl," said Sam indignantly. "I only meant you people wouldn't know her because she doesn't go in for this sort of thing."

Henry Evelyn decided that it was time to put an end to the party and the banter, good-tempered as it was. From what Horder had said to him on the telephone and from his manner now that he was in the studio, he was sure that the young man was really upset about something. He contrived to whisper as much to Vi Halliday; she nodded, then:

"Come on, Tom," she said to her husband. "How dare you stand there and let Sam insult me? Take me away from this sink of iniquity. Come, Phoebe dear," she added. "What a bore that you're taller than I am. I feel that I ought to sweep out of the room, taking you under my wing."

The others took their cue from her, and departed full of simulated wrath with Sam Horder.

"Traitor," said Phoebe Carstairs.

"Viper," said Richard Dawson.

"I say, do tell me about the tennis court at St. André," said George Appleton, whereupon the rest seized him and urged him forcibly into the hall.

Horder and Evelyn stood at the front door and watched them climb into a variety of cars and depart.

"You will show me the pictures, won't you, Sam?" was Mrs. Beecham's parting word, accompanied by her most entrancing smile.

"Say 'Yes'," shouted her husband. "I'll chaperon you."

Evelyn led the way back to the studio, closed the door, poured out two more cocktails, sat down, waved Horder to a seat and lit a cigarette.

"Sorry, old man," he said, with a sigh of relief. "They were quite peaceful till you telephoned. And I didn't like to tell 'em you really were—upset."

"That's all right, Henry, of course."

"Well, now, what is it?"

"A beastly business. Louis de Vigny is dead."

Henry Evelyn cleared his throat.

"I confess I should feel more genuinely sorry if I'd ever heard of him before," he observed.

"Sorry. I'm putting it all wrong," said Horder. "Don't you remember Margaret Daubeney?"

"Oh, of course. Yes; she married a de Vigny, didn't she?"

"Yes, but not Louis: that's her brother-in-law. Lawrence de Vigny is her husband; they own the Château St. André. You know, they're a French family, but English to all intents and purposes."

"All right. Go ahead."

"I'd forgotten all about them myself when I went to St. André. It's a quiet place, you know; 'quaint medieval relic' is the sort of thing the guidebooks say. They were very decent to me. And I met—"

"The new lady?" The architect's tone was wholly friendly and understanding.

"Yes. Verity Brown. She's—but never mind now. It was at a dance. Louis de Vigny was—murdered. Practically under my eyes. The police—well, they seemed to suspect either Margaret de Vigny or her sister Joan Daubeney. And Joan Daubeney is Verity's greatest friend. I wish to God I could help. It was—beastly. So are the police."

"Let's hear the whole story. It would do you good to get it off your chest."

"That's what I felt. That's why I rang you up. You didn't mind?"

"Of course not, old man." Henry Evelyn was some ten years the elder of the two, but he was bound closely to Horder by the memory of his sister, who had died nearly eleven years ago, just out of her teens: to this some people attributed the fact that Henry Evelyn was still a bachelor.

"You might just have a look at these sketches first," the younger man said, proffering the portfolio. "They're very rough, of course. But they may help you to understand the lie of the land. St. André is a queer old place—all heaped up like a fairy-tale castle. Wonderfully fascinating; you can easily believe that murders and tortures and battles happened there ages ago as well as Courts of Love and Troubadours—but to-day it's just a place for romance. Not for murder."

Henry Evelyn opened the portfolio.

Horder stayed to dinner, and his narrative was continued through it and afterwards. It was long afterwards, when they were settling themselves comfortably in arm-chairs that Henry Evelyn, rustling the leaves of the portfolio and turning back to the plan of the Château St. André,[1] asked whether it was "pretty accurate."

"Yes," was the reply. "I made it myself, but from an official French map. It's a Historical Monument, you know, and all that."

"H'm."

"What d'you think?" Sam asked, anxiously.

"Give me time, old man," said his friend. "As you say, it's an unpleasant business—and a puzzling one. There's this de Vigny fellow shot, with a rifle bullet, at the apex of this projecting angle of the wall—just where there is a kind of W on the plan. Oh, yes, a fire-step. So the angle of the wall gives us the limits from which the shot must have been fired. That is, either from the garden, or from the round tower—the Tour Panteleon, I see it's marked."

"Yes," said Samuel, heavily.

"And you can yourself swear that only three people were in the tower, and no one in the garden but the dead man. No one could have got to the tower without passing you?"

"Well, the people in the tower, of course, can swear that there was no one else there—I mean, otherwise someone might have gone there before I was on guard, so to speak."

"And Madame de Vigny and this big-game hunter were in the room at the top of the tower and Miss Daubeney was at the bottom of the stairs?"

"Yes."

"And none of the three had a rifle when they passed you on the way to the tower, and no rifle, or indeed any weapon at all, was discovered?"

"That's the only reason why they weren't all arrested, I think."

Henry Evelyn resumed his study of the drawings.

---

[1] Part II. No. 1.

PART TWO

THE ARTIST'S SKETCH BOOK

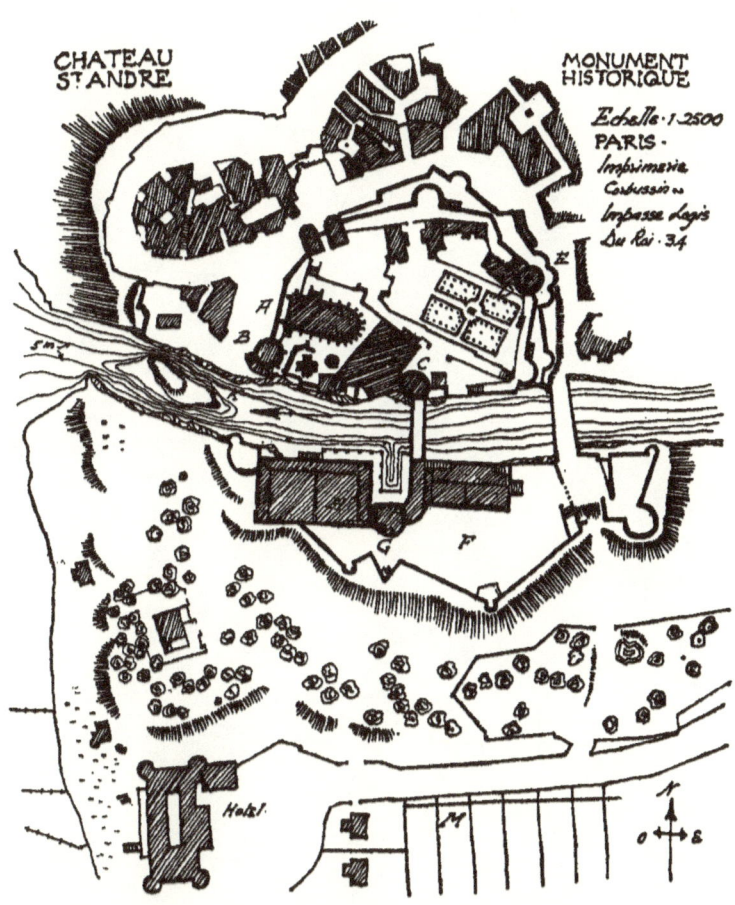

NO. I. PLAN OF THE CHÂTEAU

NO. 2. THE FLYING BRIDGE

NO. 3. TOUR PANTELEON

In the Courtyard

NO. 4. SKETCHES IN THE OLD TOWN

NO. 5. VIEW FROM THE SEA

NO. 6. CHÂTEAU FROM ABOVE SEA-SHORE

PART THREE

THE ARTIST'S STORY

CHAPTER II

SAMUEL AT ST. ANDRÉ

MR. SAMUEL HORDER, exquisite in grey flannel, artistic in a wide mauve tie, ate his solitary lunch in the Hotel Splendide at St. André-sur-mer. The garish *salle-à-manger* was nearly empty: there was no chatter and bustle to distract his meditations—which were as thoroughly mixed as his salad. Could there be anything sinister in St. André? This grotesque hotel, those jerry-built villas, the blue sea and the golden sands. And yet the hotel was only a caricature of the Château; and who knew what sinister memories lurked in the Château or in the skeleton of the Old Town clustering round its landward battlements.

Why had he come here? He found it difficult to give an honest answer even to himself. It was true his trip down the Rhône Valley had been a tourist-ridden failure; that when he fled back to Paris, he had been bored to tears; that he did really want to sketch and that he did not want to trail back to August London. And then he had heard those two Englishmen talk of St. André, as they sat at the next table in the little Paris café.

But was that the whole explanation? Of course he hadn't been—well, listening to the strangers' conversation, but all the same—it was the big man, William Burton, the one whom he had now discovered to be a big-game hunter—"Broadside Burton"; it was he who had been so set on discovering whether the mysterious, unnamed lady at St. André was being properly treated by her husband, because if she wasn't—And he had banged his big fist on the little round table. Then the little man, Kershaw, had laughed and said that if the other was set on it, he'd trail along to St. André too; if there was to be trouble he'd better be in it, though it struck him as a comic performance on his friend's part; to clear out and leave his lady-love for some absurd scruple, stay away until she'd married someone else and then come back to console her by horsewhipping the man of her choice.

Samuel Horder had to admit to himself that he had been attracted by the idea of playing the *rôle* of Observer of Life. Hadn't

Phoebe Carstairs had the cheek to tell him he knew nothing about the realities of life? . . .

Well, here he was, in this rotten hotel, with a private bathroom which he couldn't use because the water supply was short. Practically no one else here but Burton and Kershaw, though the manager declared there would be a crowd to see the Carnival—as good as the Palio at Siena or the Gipsies' Pilgrimage to Les Saintes Maries. And yet—did it matter now whether the hotel was full or empty, and whether Burton or Kershaw really was here to make trouble?

After all, had Burton meant what he said in the café? They seemed peaceful and friendly enough, he and Kershaw; they'd gone off fishing for the day. A pleasant little fellow, Kershaw; "Horace Dinnamont Kershaw, consequently called Dandy," that was how he had introduced himself that morning. His job was, it appeared, to take moving pictures of wild animals, while Burton stood beside him with a rifle in case of trouble. "Burton never misses," so Kershaw had said, grinning at the bashful giant.

When he had gone out for a stroll after dinner on the night of his arrival, Samuel thought he had run slap into Burton's mysterious "affair." It had been a queer business; he had hit by mere chance on the sandy path which ran up from the beach-road towards the little cottage with the red blind. He had walked silently up it, till he paused for breath among the trees, and then he had heard those voices. The man whispering, the woman's voice a little louder, with a hint of laughter and a hint of Cockney: "I must be quick. Good night. Good night, Lowie dear,": the sound of a kiss. He had seen the silhouette of the woman as she opened the door of the cottage; he knew now that it was the Tennis Professional's cottage and the woman, he was sure, was the Professional's wife, Mrs. Holland.

Where had the man gone? He had not passed Samuel; and he was certainly not the Pro.; Samuel had bumped into *him* at the bottom of the path as he went quietly back to the hotel; he had not on that occasion seen Holland's face, though the man had seen his— the lighting of a cigarette had not served Sam's purpose. But on the beach this morning, Holland had recognized him and spoken to him. He was a grim, dark man, with the figure and muscles of the trained athlete; but his rough voice was surely not the one which had whispered among the trees. Besides, why whisper to his wife? And his name seemed to be Leonard.

A handsome woman, Mrs. Holland, and she had a marvelous figure—of which she certainly was not ashamed. Hadn't she been careful to throw on her wrap close by where Sam had been sitting this morning, and flash her eyes at him and . . .?

But what did it all matter? Sam recurred to the topic which was foremost in his thoughts: Verity Brown. What luck that he had got up so early. Of course he had really meant to bathe before breakfast, but—well, the air had been cool, and if his artistic eye had not been delighted by the slim, solitary figure in the red bathing dress, standing in the edge of the sea, hesitating . . .

Sam's cheeks reddened. Had he made an awful fool of himself? He had meant to dash into the sea, calling out a casual sort of "Good morning" as he passed the girl, and later on . . . But he had not realized how quickly the beach shelved down; his headlong tumble had splashed the girl from head to foot and she had, beyond all doubt, sworn at him in return. Still, that was surely forgotten. It had been jolly sporting of her to come after him to warn him about bathing at high tide and the danger of getting the wrong side of the groin; Samuel felt a little guilty when he remembered how she had thanked him for hauling her back to dry land. It had been an awkward minute or two; she had jolly nearly got swept across the groin, and he had felt quite shaken. So had she, poor girl, not to speak of the scratches she'd got from the timbers and iron uprights.

By Jove, she was certainly pretty; of course he had recognized her at once as the girl he had admired so much at that Hunt Ball. And she had been rather pleased, and quite ready to talk. And when he learnt that she was staying at the Château and that the chatelaine, Margaret de Vigny, had been a Miss Daubeney, and that she and Sam had lots of acquaintances in common—well, he knew that he had fallen in clover.

He hoped that Miss Brown—he was already calling her "Verity" to himself—had taken as swift a liking to him as he to her. Or was it just because the party at the Château was a badly balanced one? M. de Vigny and his wife, Louis de Vigny and Madame de Vigny's sister Joan Daubeney (that was Verity's real friend, of course)—the four made the family party, and Verity was odd girl out. Or was Joan the odd girl out, or did Verity, at any rate, want her to play that *rôle?*

Samuel frowned. It had been very jolly to join the Château party when they came down to bathe later in the morning; and they did it handsomely too, with the big Renault and the ample supply of cocktails.

Only—well, the atmosphere had been a bit difficult. Of course he had realized that it could not have been Burton who had been whispering among the trees; for when he had had those few words alone with the big-game hunter after breakfast and had spoken of his acquaintance with one of the Château party (he had not mentioned how very newly formed it was), the other had asked him not to mention the name of Burton to any of the party. "An old friend—Of course I shall eventually go and call—But Kershaw and I want a quiet change first—Don't want to offend them by seeming to neglect our Social Duties." The big man had blushed so deeply that Sam was quite sure that Madame de Vigny was the lady of his romance. Besides, when Burton and Kershaw had gone off in their boat and the Tennis Professional and his wife came down to bathe close to where Sam was basking in the sun, he had, he was sure, recognized her voice as the one which had said good night to "Lowie."

It was when he had been introduced to the Château party by Verity—who seemed to have given a glowing account of his before-breakfast prowess—and when he had found it difficult to find anything to talk about, that he had made some reference to the two English people whom he had just been speaking to—the good-looking woman and her husband. There had been that awkward pause—very awkward—whilst the others all avoided catching one another's eyes. By Jove, he saw what a fool he had been—it must have been Louis de Vigny who—

It was Lawrence de Vigny who had come to the rescue. "That must have been Mr. and Mrs. Holland—he is my Tennis Professional," he had said, in a level, colourless tone, and he had gone on to talk about the game and his interest in it, and the number of years for which there had been a tennis-court at St. André—oh, long before the present one was built, or adapted from an old warehouse on the banks of the stream which ran through the Château. Once it had been the main river, but by degrees the other branch had usurped its place, and the New Town had grown up on its far banks; so that now the Old River was as much a picturesque antiquity as the Old Town, though a much more lively one—a fierce torrent running between high cliffs and dividing the Château proper from the outwork which to-day included the tennis-court and the vegetable garden, and spanned by the famous "flying bridge."

"You must come and see it, Mr. Horder," M. de Vigny had concluded, courteously, and his wife had seconded the invitation.

Well, they had bathed and sat about and drunk cocktails and the rest of the morning had gone by pleasantly enough—with a friendly look, too, in Verity's eye. And when they all packed themselves into the Renault, Lawrence de Vigny had told him he could come up to the Château whenever he liked, to sketch, and he thought that he read a silent support of the invitation in Verity's glance; and then Margaret de Vigny had gone one better, suggesting that he should join them again next morning for a bathe and go back to lunch with them afterwards.

So Samuel had gone back to the hotel feeling quite pleased with life. It was only when he began to think things over that he felt that there were currents below the surface.

There was Burton—or rather there he wasn't, as he and Kershaw were somewhere picnicking at sea or on the island in the bay; however, the fact remained that he had been almost *too* careful not to mention him to the de Vignys. And it was not only about the Burton affair that he felt uneasy.

Oh, they had all been charming enough; and though Verity Brown's looks were the sort that appealed to him (or so he felt suddenly convinced), Joan Daubeney too was pretty and nice; Verity with her dark Eton cropped head, and those level grey eyes and the curious narrow eyebrows, a steady, far-seeing look, and Joan with her fair fluffy hair and bright blue eyes . . . Margaret de Vigny must have been very pretty, too, but she looked a good deal older than her sister.

When he contemplated this aspect of the Château party, his feeling that St. André was a jolly place began to revive; in spite of the ugly, empty hotel. All the same it was queer that they had welcomed him so warmly. Verity, of course—well, he thought he had got on with her from the first. But why had the others—sort of jumped at him?

Margaret de Vigny, to begin with. She had been friendly enough—though they had all been that. And of course the fact of their having mutual acquaintances had helped. But there appeared to be something on her mind; she was a little aloof, even in her tone to her husband, and she seemed to watch her sister Joan with rather a cold eye. Was that why *she* had welcomed him? Because he was a potential counter-attraction to Louis de Vigny? It had certainly seemed to Samuel that Louis either was in the middle of a vigorous flirtation with Joan Daubeney or else that he would like to start one.

What else was there about Louis? At first his manner towards the new-comer had not been particularly enthusiastic but later on it had changed. Why was that? Samuel pondered, and decided with a gentle blush, that it was because he and Verity Brown obviously were—well, friendly; he reverted to his theory of Verity as "odd girl out." Louis hadn't liked it when Joan had welcomed the new-comer with open arms; but afterwards he had realized that there were advantages in balancing the party. If Verity was occupied with the artist—that left Louis with only Joan to look after.

That would explain Joan, too; on the assumption, of course, that whether or not the flirtation had actually started, she had no objection to such a diversion.

The hardest to understand was Lawrence de Vigny. He seemed so bored and uninterested. Quite polite, but no more until he suddenly brightened up. Why, yes, that was when the subject of tennis had come up. He had been so hopeful that Samuel knew how to play, and very scornful when the latter had thought that he was referring to lawn tennis and not to the "real" game. Said he was bored with playing with no one but his brother and the professional. And at that there had been another queer moment of constraint: ended by some light-hearted remark by Louis, who had flung a friendly, mocking look at his brother. Was Samuel being too sensitive to the atmosphere? After all, the de Vignys were thoroughly English, in spite of their French name and possessions and so forth; there was nothing unreasonable in their being glad to chance upon a presentable young Englishman on holiday, with the right sort of connexions. And besides he just balanced the party.

Yet he couldn't dismiss the idea that there were strange undercurrents. It was a pity, in a way, that he didn't play real tennis; it might have helped him to get inside the two de Vignys' guard, so to speak—you can do that more easily when you play a game with a man than in any other way, he reflected. Yes, he was sure that there was something peculiar about those two men. There must have been, or Margaret de Vigny would not have kept a critical eye (as he judged it) on that flirtation. Was that all there was to it? That Lawrence de Vigny would have no objection to a marriage between Louis and Joan, but that Margaret had quite other views on the subject?

Samuel suddenly remembered the couple by the cottage last night. Was *that* it? Light broke in on his musings. If they were

Mrs. Holland and Louis . . . Probably Louis's brother knew all about that little affair, and Margaret too; and Lawrence's French blood, as well as his affection for his brother, led to his seeing nothing particularly objectionable in it. Yes, that would explain a lot.

Samuel's meditations occupied him throughout his lunch, a meal to which he did full justice; they lasted beyond his coffee, taken in the shade of the veranda. The afternoon seemed even hotter than the morning, and St. André more deserted than ever. There was such a glare from the sea and the sand and white road that Samuel closed his eyes, and slept. . . .

CHAPTER III

OLD FRIENDS MEET

Someone was creeping stealthily towards him . . . yes, it was the man he had heard by the cottage, but whose face he hadn't seen. And still he could not see it—the man as he crawled kept his hand up, like a lady screening her cheeks from a hot wood fire. Now he was crouching for a leap—now his fingers were clawing Sam's shoulder, clawing towards his throat, and the man's face—God, he hadn't got a face at all—only the bare grinning skull . . .

Sam struggled desperately—and opened his eyes to find Dandy Kershaw standing over him and watching him with a grim smile.

"What—what the devil . . .?" Sam began, in bewilderment.

"Pardon the liberty, as they say," Kershaw interrupted. "I woke you up because you were snoring—like the devil you referred to."

"Snoring!" Sam expressed the infuriated incredulity which we all feel at the one accusation which none of us can ever satisfactorily meet—"I never snore."

"My God," Kershaw retorted. "All I can say is that I thought to myself that the sea fog comes down pretty quickly here."

The artist, with as good a grace as he could manage, combined an apology for himself with a pardon for Kershaw.

"It's all this bathing and sea air—and food," he added, and Kershaw took him severely to task for his indolence. It appeared that he and Burton had had a thoroughly energetic day—to Sam's astonishment it was going on for four o'clock—though they'd caught no fish to speak of.

"And where's Mr. Burton?" Sam inquired idly; partly to divert the conversation into another channel. He did not want to show resentment at the impertinence of this stranger in criticizing him.

"Oh, he's gone to have a look at the Old Town. Old Broadside Burton's no stickler for appearances. He was hot when he got back and he reckoned he'd get hot walking about among the ruins, so he saw no point in changing. Personally, what I really like best about a spell of idleness in Europe is to feel that clothes do matter after all," and a shade complacently he adjusted his dapper bow tie.

There was a short pause, then:

"I suppose you don't feel like a walk?" Kershaw went on. "I thought of going in pursuit of Burton, so to speak."

"To the Old Town? Yes, rather."

Sam rose to his feet, yawned and grinned apologetically.

"I'd certainly better do something to work off the effects of my doze," he added.

"Doze," said Kershaw. "My holy aunt, if that's a doze—I hope your room's some way away from mine. Come on, then."

They set out, taking the road along which Samuel had been driven by the bus from the station the previous day. Kershaw set the pace, and made it rather brisker than his companion could have wished but he was afraid to say so. Evidently he was already an object of pity, all because of that doze on the veranda. Kershaw indeed remarked that in addition to his desire for companionship, he had felt obliged to wake the sleeper for the sake of their country's reputation.

They soon turned off from the main road, and took another, narrower and more primitive, a track rather than a road, which joined it from the left. Clearly it was a short cut to the Old Town—probably the old road, only lately deposed from its place of honour as a result of the "development" projects.

The track ran fairly straight to the belt of trees on the rising ground below the Château. Samuel caught a glimpse, to his left, of that cottage with the red blind. Beyond the trees they came into full view of the Château, or rather of the bridge-head on the south side of the "old" river. Grim walls, sheer and battlemented, crowned the steep slope, or perhaps converted it into an artificial cliff, for the track ran so sharply up to what evidently was a breach in the walls that it was easy to judge that the ground level inside the walls of the bridge-head was much higher than outside.

Within the breach, and to the right, the last few yards of the wall met the river bank at a sharp angle, turned and ran back to meet an ugly bridge. The little corner was covered with worn burnt grass and in it was a large seat of weathered stone. To the left were tall iron railings—tall and spiked—and through them the two men had a view of a kitchen garden (though mysteriously known to antiquity as the *Râteau de Bœuf),* bounded by the outer wall on one side and on the other by massive buildings into which a curious tower was confusingly built.

"If they can afford to have their kitchen garden *there,*" Sam remarked to Kershaw, "the rest of the Château must be even more marvelous than I supposed."

"I expect you'll soon be able to judge for yourself?"

"Oh, yes. I'm lunching there, to-morrow, I think."

Kershaw grunted. They were by now crossing the narrow bridge—a modern affair, whose parapets were so high that the pedestrian, at all events, was virtually in blinkers.

"Evidently they don't like strangers to overlook them," was Kershaw's comment, and Samuel agreed that the parapet robbed them of a striking view; the gorge through which the river ran, cutting off the bridge-head from the Château proper, must, he thought, be very well worth seeing.

"But I expect we shall both of us be able to judge for ourselves very soon," he added.

Kershaw looked at him sharply and questioningly. He felt constrained to explain that Burton had told him of his former acquaintance with Madame de Vigny—and then he had a horrible qualm, for he was not sure whether Burton had gone quite as far as that. But Kershaw, of course, had no views either way, and seemed rather relieved that Sam knew so much.

"Burton's a queer fellow," he said. "Suffers from a misplaced modesty. But a damned good man to have beside you in a crisis, with a gun in his hand."

Beyond the bridge, a precipitous cliff bounded the road on the left and the towers and pinnacles of the Château sprang fantastically skywards from its summit. Ahead and to the right was the Old Town, into whose bleached ruins the track, thick in white sandy dust, abruptly plunged. They followed it round the foot of the cliff, and soon they came to a flight of steps running up the side of the cliff, a medieval side-door to the Château, perhaps; and just opposite this point a particularly alluring alley ran down hill, away from the Château, into the heart of the Old Town.

"Let's try that," Samuel almost shouted, and suited his action to the word.

Kershaw hesitated.

"Don't want to miss Burton," he muttered. And then with, "Oh well, we'll probably miss him whichever way we go," he followed the other's lead.

"Behaves like a nursemaid or the keeper of a lunatic," Samuel thought to himself, rather annoyed. "This Burton fellow is surely capable of finding his way home by himself."

He hurried on, in an excitement of delight; a low archway caught his eye, and what looked like a little green courtyard beyond it. He turned aside and went in, Kershaw at his heels—and almost collided with a couple who apparently were on the point of emerging. In the dust, a footfall made no sound.

"Oh, *pardon,*" began Sam, in his best French accent, and then stopped short, feeling rather foolish at the sight of Margaret de Vigny and Mr. William Burton.

"Why, hullo!" he said, addressing the lady, and Kershaw greeted the man with similar inanity.

"Why, it's Mr. Horder," said Margaret de Vigny. She sounded quite breathless. "And is this your friend Mr. Kershaw?" she asked Burton.

The big man pulled himself together—he looked both startled and suspicious—and effected a formal introduction. Margaret de Vigny looked at Samuel and evidently decided that some kind of explanation was called for.

"Wasn't it strange, Mr. Horder?" she said. "Mr. Burton's a very old friend of mine whom I've not seen for years and I bump into him in this tumble-down place."

"I told Horder this morning—" Burton put in ill-advisedly.

"He never said a word about your being here," she spoke and looked reproachfully at Samuel, and to the general embarrassment Burton was obliged to explain that the reticence had been at his request.

Samuel was rather annoyed to feel that the atmosphere was one of guilt—guilt on the part of Burton and the lady for having been encountered, and on the others' part for having blundered into them. Kershaw came to the rescue by announcing, quite untruly, that the artist had particularly wanted to see something of the Old Town at once; and the net result was that, the blind leading the blind, the two of them had got lost in a couple of minutes.

Margaret de Vigny, still with a tired and strained expression in her eyes, observed that she knew her way pretty well in the maze, and would gladly conduct them on a short tour.

She was as good as her word, and made a very efficient guide; but it was useless to pretend that the tour was a success or that the attention even of that enthusiastic artist, Mr. Samuel Horder, was really on the beauties of architecture and of Nature which they surveyed. They talked loudly of the beauties of the scene, as if hoping to force their thoughts into the same channel. Kershaw was a tower of strength.

They had walked through devious and intricate ways before suddenly they emerged up a flight of crumbling stone steps upon the continuation of the track from St. André-sur-Mer: here no longer a humble track but forking into a well-kept road, winding narrowly but boldly round the steep cliff on one side up to the main gate of the Château, and on the other sweeping down towards the "new" river and a yet newer bridge which spanned it. The wharves and roofs and spires of the "new St. André"—the town of which St. André-sur-Mer was an incipient adjunct—lay in full view.

Kershaw, with Sam at his heels, emerged upon the road. The other two paused a moment, and Sam, listening in defiance of his better feelings, seemed to catch a murmured word or two, "to-morrow morning" and "courtyard."

An angry roar was followed by the sudden appearance of the Renault round the corner of a building. The driver caught sight of them and drew up, with a reckless indifference to the effect on the brakes. It was Lawrence de Vigny, alone.

"Hullo!" he said. "Been paying a call? Sorry we were all out. I've just been down to the town."

Precisely at that moment Margaret de Vigny and Burton stepped up into the road; they could not, of course, have seen the car, and it seemed that they had been too deep in conversation to notice the noise of its approach; indeed, Margaret's hand was resting on Burton's arm and—

"Hullo!" said Lawrence again, a new inflexion in his voice. His wife's cheeks which had had some colour in them for the first time since Sam had met her ("Those steps, no doubt," he thought to himself) went white again.

"Hullo, Margaret. Want a lift?"

"You're very opportune, Lawrence," she replied, composedly enough. "Both with the car, and because I want to introduce you to a very old friend of mine—Bill Burton. I'm sure you've heard me talk of him."

Lawrence's eyes narrowed, and Burton's opened rather wide: you might have thought that they were two peculiar varieties of the same wild animal.

"I have indeed," was his answer, in a tone with which no fault could be found; and then he added, with a suspicion of a sneer, "and I'm delighted to meet you at last."

Burton muttered some kind of reply. Kershaw was then introduced and was favoured with a very keen scrutiny and a very brilliant "social" smile.

"Wasn't it a bit of luck that I ran into Bill?" Margaret addressed her husband.

"Rather," said he. "Quite a family party."

Sam felt that the five of them would stay forever at those crossroads saying nothing in particular.

"I say, we ought to be getting back to the hotel, I suppose?" he said.

"Ah, you're staying down here?" Lawrence asked Burton. "That's capital. We must fix something up. Margaret'll be sure to see you to-morrow—or I will."

As he spoke he opened the door of the car. His wife got in. There was a general chorus of "Good night"; a wave of the hand from Lawrence and the car shot off, raising a cloudy swirl of dust.

The three men watched it for a few seconds till it went out of sight round a bend in the road, then turned and started on their walk home.

"We must have been longer than I thought, wandering about." Samuel addressed no one in particular, and proceeded to embark upon a long eulogy of the charms of the Old Town.

He got singularly little help from his two companions, one of whom seemed moody and depressed, and at the same time (if his sudden frowns were a sure guide) rather angry, whilst Dandy Kershaw was manifestly anxious about his friend's thoughts and feelings. After some time, Samuel's unaided powers began to fail. The walk finished in heavy silence.

CHAPTER IV

THE ROYAL GAME OF TENNIS

NEXT MORNING Sam and Verity repeated their before-breakfast bathe but with variations. There was no life-saving this time; the breeze was colder, the bathe shorter, the conversation longer, and then the girl departed up the path to the Hollands' cottage—a short cut to the Château via the tennis-court, it seemed. As there was no longer any secret about the presence of Burton and Kershaw, Samuel suggested to Verity that she might care to pass on the discovery which he had made overnight at dinner, that Kershaw had once been a real-tennis player and would enjoy a game. Verity jumped at the idea—it might be a godsend to the de Vignys; she was so pleased with Sam that she let him know that he was to be invited to join the Château party for the Carnival, "A dinner and dance at the Château and then go and look at the people in fancy dress in the Old Town."

Sam was highly gratified, and when after breakfast he heard the *concierge* announcing (in a tone of mingled pride and deference) that a messenger had brought a note from the Château, he felt sure that it was his invitation. But he was wrong; it was for Kershaw, who was standing beside him.

Kershaw tore it open.

"Now how the devil did he know that?" he asked, and tossed the note to Horder so carelessly that the *concierge* looked positively shocked.

"DEAR MR. KERSHAW (Sam read),

"I hear that you are—or were—a tennis player. Do make use of the court here. It is such a pleasure to find fresh opponents. Why not come up at about half-past ten this morning? We can fit you out with any gear you need.

"Yours sincerely,

"LAWRENCE DE VIGNY."

The young man, rather red in the face, explained that he had mentioned tennis-playing to one of the house-party.

"The charming young lady with whom you went bathing this morning?" Kershaw suggested with a twinkling eye, and Sam's deepening colour was sufficient answer. "Well," he continued, "it is a good many years since I played the game, but as Burton's gone off and left me in the lurch and you probably have numerous and attractive plans for the morning, and as I get bored if I am left to my own company, I may as well take him at his word. It's a long walk, though, isn't it? He might have sent the car."

"There's a P.S.," said Sam—he had only just noticed it, on the other side of the sheet of note-paper. "It says that the tennis court door will be open. It's no distance that way—I'll walk up with you if you like. I've never seen the game played, so it would be interesting."

Kershaw agreed. They sat for a minute or two on the veranda and then the other man departed in search of suitable attire. "Hope they won't turn up their noses at my sand-shoes," he said; "I got 'em at the café. Not what I'd call smart."

They started in good time, since Samuel really had little idea of the distance. And when they reached the point where the path turned towards the cottage, he hesitated. He hardly liked to walk up to the front door and into the garden. At that moment, however, Mrs, Holland came out and saw them. There was something gipsy-like in her dress and appearance, and the artist could not help feeling that she would be a good subject for a portrait.

She beamed upon them. "Looking for the tennis-court?" she asked in that curious accent. "Len—that's my husband—said that a gentleman from the hotel would most likely be going up to play this morning. It's straight through the garden here," she continued, when Sam replied in the affirmative. "Through that gate the other side; then just follow the path."

She moved close to Sam and pointed out the way. Her hand flashed in the sunshine. They thanked her. "Lovely day again," she said, displaying a desire to linger.

Again Sam assented; Kershaw said nothing.

"Well, see you bathing later, I expect," she went on, apparently deciding that the moment was not after all opportune to extend the acquaintance. "Have a good game," she added, addressing Kershaw and glancing at the shoes which he carried in his hand.

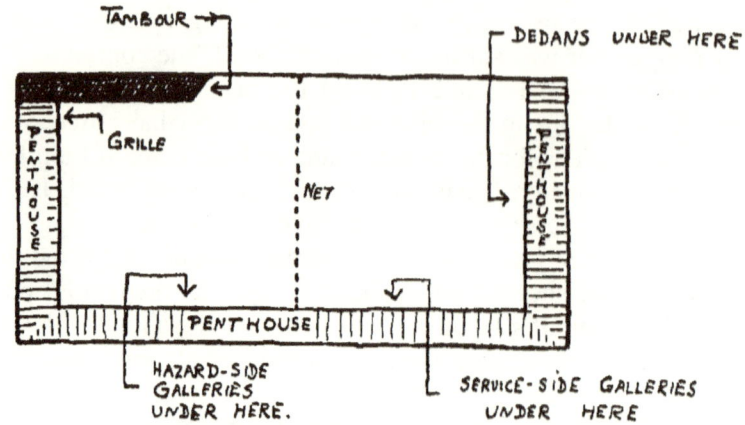

I. ROUGH PLAN OF TENNIS-COURT

Facsimile of Mr. G. Appleton's diagram to illustrate his explanation of the game of tennis.

They reiterated their thanks and walked on through the garden.

"And who's *that?*" asked Kershaw, as he paused to shut the gate behind him. "You seem to be making plenty of hay, my lad."

"Oh, the wife of the tennis pro.," Sam told him, indifferently. "I've never spoken to her before but she was pointed out to me—"

"Must be a paying job," Kershaw observed. "See her rings?"

"Oh, Woolworth's, I expect."

"Don't you believe it. Damn pretty woman, too. Australian, I should think, eh? *And* not so slow either."

Sam's manner was intended to convey his opinion of his companion's vulgarity. All that it produced however was a quiet chuckle.

Conversation languished, for they were confronted with a sharp climb. At this end the wall of the bridgehead had been used to form part of a large edifice rather suggestive of a barrack. The path ended in a flight of steps and a doorway, of recent date, cut in the wall.

"I suppose this is it," said Sam, trying the handle. The door was unlocked and he stepped into what he later discovered was called the "dedans."

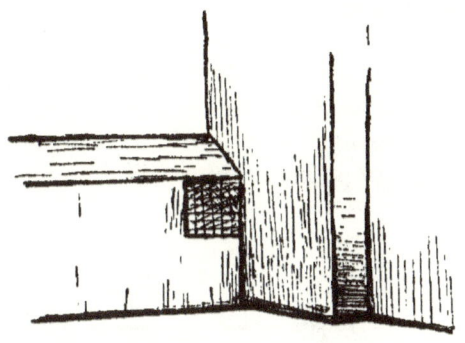

II. ROUGH SKETCH OF GRILLE AND TAMBOUR

Mr. G. Appleton's diagram.

In the St. André court little provision was made for spectators. The dedans in fact was little wider than the penthouse. Sam jumped as a ball landed with a thud on the penthouse overhead and Kershaw laughed. Through the netting in front of the dedans they could see the players—Lawrence de Vigny and (as Sam knew) Holland, the professional. Lawrence was on the far (or "hazard') side of the court. The professional waited for the ball to bound on the roof, and then, stooping in the orthodox fashion, and wearing an expression suggestive of medieval ruthlessness, smote it severely and accurately against a brown square on the far wall. There was a resounding thud.

"Good shot," said Kershaw, and to Sam, "that's the grille"—as if thereby everything was explained.

The professional turned and said "Good morning," in a civil tone, and to his opponent, "The two gentlemen, sir."

It struck Samuel that the man contrived to make the "sir" almost insulting. De Vigny however appeared to notice nothing peculiar.

"Two!" he said, advancing to the net. He came along by the side gallery to greet them.

"Very glad you've come," he said cordially to Kershaw. "My brother's too preoccupied to play much, and Holland's too damned good. I want a game, not a lesson."

Kershaw remarked drily that as he hadn't played for donkeys' years he probably could not give him what he wanted.

"Rot," said de Vigny. "I'm no good. You'll only want a spot of practice. Hullo, sorry. I didn't notice who it was," he went on to Sam. "I thought you said you didn't play?"

"I don't," the young man replied. "I just showed Kershaw the way up and I thought perhaps you wouldn't mind if I watched."

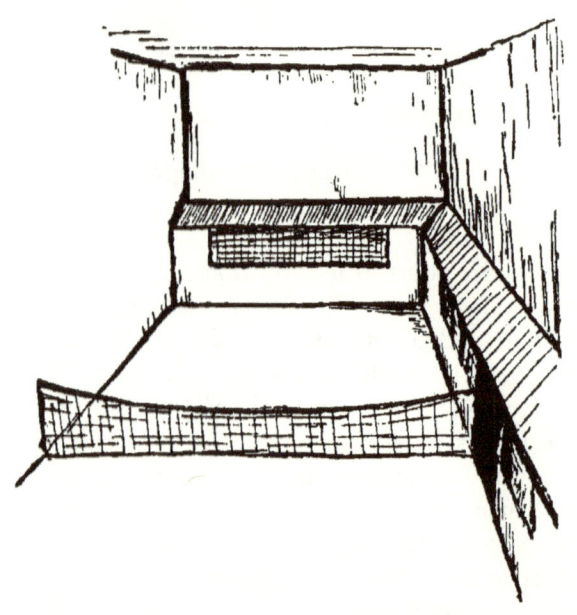

3   ROUGH SKETCH · OF SERVICE-SIDE OF COURT

Mr. G. Appleton's Diagram.

"Delighted, my dear man, though you'll find it devilish dull if you don't understand the rules. Still, the others will probably drift down before long, if only to drag me away for the scheduled bathe."

He looked at Sam maliciously.

"I'm not sure that Miss Brown can teach you much about this game, though," he added; there was just enough stress on the word "this" to give it a special meaning without making it reasonable to take offence.

"Come on, put your shoes on," he continued to Kershaw, before either man could answer. "You and I'll have a knock-up—just to get your muscles loose."

Kershaw sat down and removed his coat and scarf and shoes, and donned the local production with a word of apology for their shape and appearance. De Vigny meanwhile called to Holland to bring along some racquets, and discoursed about the court—its pace and peculiarities.

Kershaw selected a racquet from a number which the professional offered him and followed his host into the court. Sam had rather counted upon the professional explaining the game to him, but he took up his position in the marker's box and the artist was left to his own resources. At intervals Kershaw, who was on his side of the court, made some remark to him, or to de Vigny, apologizing for his inability to hit the ball; Sam gathered that they were knocking up. "You'll have to give me half a dozen bisques," Kershaw called out to his antagonist, who replied, "Oh, it'll soon come back. I'll give you fifteen to start with and then we'll see." They continued to strike the ball, as far as Sam could judge, in a perfectly aimless manner, and then he suddenly gathered that the game had started; Holland was intoning the score, though in a manner which made it quite impossible for the solitary spectator to know what was happening. For he was not aware either that service does not automatically change at the end of a game, or that the score called first is not the server's, as in lawn-tennis, but that of the winner of the last point. And then all of a sudden the two players began to exchange sides of the net with absurd frequency. Sam began to feel not only bewildered but bored. And it was almost chilly in the dark gallery where he sat.

As quietly as he could—with needless quiet, since the other three were all concentrated on the game—he made his way along the gallery below the side penthouse (much intrigued by the further network from which he could still watch the game) and round the other end. The passage below the far penthouse was almost pitch dark, having, of course, no opening into the court. He groped his way however to a crack of light and discovered it to be a door. He opened it and stepped out on to what seemed the edge of a miniature dock, in size not unlike those in the gardens along the banks of the Thames. A flat stone path, a couple of yards wide ran round its three land-bound sides; an iron railing guarded the unwary from walking into the water, and at intervals graceful pillars supported a light roof which converted the path into a colonnade. He leant on the railing and looked up. Nearly overhead, the flying bridge leapt across the gorge of the river, ending in a tower on the other side. The river ran silent and cold past the beetling cliff.

"By Jove!" thought Sam to himself, "this *is* worth seeing, this Château."

From an open door in the colonnade on the opposite side of the dock came the sound of voices and laughter. Joan Daubeney appeared, Verity Brown and Louis de Vigny close behind her. All three wore bathing wraps.

"Well, well," she said, as she caught sight of Samuel, "you do get about the place, don't you?"

He advanced to meet them, and hastily explained his presence.

"What a marvelous place this is," he added.

"Sorry our play wasn't exciting enough," a voice said behind him, and he turned to find Lawrence de Vigny. He looked so startled that the latter apologized.

"It's the fault of my rubber shoes," he explained with a smile.

"Coming to bathe, Lawrence?" Joan demanded. "And what about you, Mr. Horder?"

"Yes, I'll come," Lawrence answered. "Just give me a couple of minutes to change my shoes. Aren't we going by car though?"

Before anyone could answer his question however, he went on to Samuel, "Your Mr. Kershaw insists on having a bit of practice with Holland. Of course, he's right out of practice, so——"

"Don't say you've found someone you can beat, Lawrence," Joan flung at him. "Poor Mr. Kershaw! He'll have to play you day and night, won't he?"

There was a cold anger in her brother-in-law's eyes, though he managed to laugh naturally enough.

"Thanks, Joan," he said. "But, I say, what about the car? We don't want to toil down on foot, do we?"

It was Louis who answered, and Sam, who was facing him squarely across the little strip of dark water, noticed that his face wore a suspicion of a sneer—and yet there was something of amusement, too, in his expression.

"Didn't you know?" he asked his brother. "Magneto. No Renault till this afternoon. Of course if you like to go in the two-seater while we walk—"

"Oh, no, I'll walk too. We can go down by the path," Lawrence answered easily. "Come and see the changing rooms," he added to Sam, and led the way past the other three and through the doorway out of which they had emerged.

"The only objection," he observed in reply to the artist's enthusiasm for the spot, "is that it's quite a tricky walk from the house to the court. This is the only way."

They ascended a short flight of stairs, to a wide landing—it might properly be called a gallery. Its tall windows overlooked the river, and looked up to the Château walls and the flying bridge. The bridge indeed entered the building in which Sam found himself, becoming an open gallery reached from the one in which he stood by the continuation of the staircase which he had ascended. To the right was a wall with two doors in it, and containing two rooms equipped as changing rooms. At the far end of the gallery yet another staircase descended straight to a door; this gave admission to the kitchen garden, roughly opposite to the tall iron railings which Kershaw and he had passed on their way to the Old Town. This door, as Samuel subsequently learnt, was always kept locked.

The gallery or landing in which he sat on a comfortable sofa and waited whilst Lawrence de Vigny changed was in fact a sort of key position. Apart from the postern gate by which he had entered, it afforded the only means of access to the tennis-court; and the only way of reaching the court from the Château was through it. Finally the only way from the Château to the curious round tower which he and Kershaw had noticed the previous evening (the door of which was in turn the normal way of entering the kitchen garden) also ran across it, in full view of anyone seated on Sam's sofa.

Lawrence de Vigny reappeared, clad in a bath-wrap, and apologized for keeping the artist waiting.

"I thought one of the others would have come up to entertain you," he said, "but Kershaw seems to have been a strong counter-attraction. Unless they've walked on down to the shore."

Sam's reply was to refer to the attractions of the gallery.

"Pleasant, isn't it?" the owner agreed. "Used to be a warehouse. So was the tennis-court. They said I ought to pull 'em both down because they spoil the tower but I didn't see my way to do that. I mean to say, they mayn't be as old as the tower and they mayn't have such a jolly name—Panteleon's Tower, it's called—but they're a good deal older than I am—and I like my game of tennis."

He led the way back to the tennis-court, round the little dock. Kershaw and the professional were still hard at it, and in the dedans Louis and the two girls were making a show of interest in the game. Lawrence did not seem overjoyed at seeing them there.

"Come along," he said. "Let's have our bathe, and leave Kershaw to it. Oh yes, he said he'd like to."

"Keep him busy, then, Holland," Louis called laughingly to the players. Kershaw, very hot but full of enthusiasm, waved his racquet in reply; the professional's scowl deepened as he delivered a fast and accurate American service with which Kershaw could do nothing at all.

CHAPTER V

THE ACCEPTANCE OF INVITATIONS

THEY FILED merrily and rapidly down the path. Louis seemed in high spirits and when level ground was reached he took the lead, Samuel coming next. He opened the gate of the cottage garden and went ahead; Sam politely held it open and so relegated himself to the tail of the procession. Beyond the cottage the order of marching became: Louis an easy first; then Joan, closely followed by Lawrence; another but smaller gap and then Verity and Sam. The leader gave a sudden shout and broke into a run.

"Hi! Mrs. Holland!"

Another white-robed figure had come into view farther down the path. At the shout she stopped and turned. Sam's view was partly obscured by those in front, but it seemed to him that her smile was more reserved, or less confident, than when she had greeted Kershaw and himself.

"Going to join the parade, or insist on having your own private Lido?"

Her reply was not audible at the tail of the procession, but two things were certain—that Verity, with an exclamation, hurried on past Lawrence and came up with Joan, and that Lawrence swore loudly and in a savage tone described his brother as a—fool.

Louis smilingly in conversation with Mrs. Holland was blissfully unaware of the effect of his words. As the others came up he turned to them gaily and cried:

"She will! A new recruit."

Nothing was said until the road was reached, and there Mrs. Holland dropped back so that the two girls had to draw abreast of her. They greeted her politely, but coldly; there was a note of defiant apology in the way in which she returned their greeting.

Sam felt indignant at such snobbery; deliberately he joined them and grinned at Mrs. Holland in his friendliest way.

"We're always meeting, aren't we?" he said.

She looked at him from the corners of her magnificent eyes—gratefully, but provocatively.

"Oh, but aren't you bathing, Mr.—?"

"Horder," he supplied. "Yes, rather. I'll skip along to the hotel and change."

"Good morning, Mrs. Holland," Lawrence's cold voice broke in. "So you're going to join us, eh?"

"I should love to. Len's up at the court, isn't he? I thought he was playing *with you.* "

Their eyes met in what Samuel felt to be a duel. He noticed, too, the professional's wife omitted the "sir" as pointedly as her husband used it.

"It's dull bathing alone, isn't it?" she added, and turned to put her question directly to Verity Brown, who was saved the necessity of answering by Louis, now waiting for them on the sands; he shouted something about "Don't be in a hurry to bathe. I'll be back in a minute," and then set off briskly in the direction of the hotel. Samuel felt thoroughly ill at ease and was glad to have a good reason for pursuing Louis. Perhaps the awkwardness would have worn off by the time he had changed.

"Hurry up," Verity called, and his heart smote him and he abandoned the idea of taking a long time; he suddenly felt that he was deserting her, snobbery or no snobbery. By Jove, though, it might not be snobbery at all; he'd forgotten those voices in the night. Louis de Vigny and Mrs. Holland! No wonder that Verity had hurried to overtake Joan and that Lawrence—

Louis had a good start, and he emerged from the hotel as Sam reached it. With him came the *concierge* protesting volubly that he could perfectly well manage it all by himself—"it" being a large luncheon-basket. The breakdown of the Renault clearly was not to be permitted to spoil the ritual of the bathe. Louis repeated Verity's injunction to hurry.

The contents of the basket helped the cause of amity, though the bathing parade was hardly as successful as the first which Sam had attended. Lawrence, however, had cheered up and congratulated his brother on his foresight.

"Thank Margaret, too," said the latter; and Sam hoped that her absence would now be explained.

"Margaret?" her husband echoed in some surprise. "But I thought she'd gone to St. André."

"So she has. And in the two-seater. Just as well you decided of your own free will to walk, wasn't it?" (That amused sneer made its reappearance.) "But she came down to the hotel first—left your note for Kershaw and the basket for us."

"I wonder whether Burton—" Sam began, and wished he had bitten out his tongue, such were the looks he received from Joan and Verity. Mrs. Holland, who was sitting on the sands with her cloak skilfully draped to suggest modesty without ensuring it, looked interested and puzzled at the abrupt cessation of his wonder.

"When in doubt, bathe," said Lawrence de Vigny, abruptly, and did so. The rest followed his example. Sam contrived to whisper to Verity:

"I'm awfully sorry if I put my foot in it. What *is* it all about?"

"Oh, nothing much. But the less said sooner mended."

Though the wind had dropped, the water was still colder than it had been the morning before. They all agreed that a short, sharp swim was the order of the day. Joan Daubeney seemed to have lost all her high spirits, and was the first to return to dry land. It was as the rest of them waded up the beach after her that the last and (Sam felt) most significant incident happened. He himself was standing in a couple of feet of water waiting for the others to overtake him. Mrs. Holland and Lawrence de Vigny were four or five yards from him when the former suddenly stumbled and fell practically into Lawrence's arms. In a moment she was wading on again with a laughing apology; yet in that moment Samuel would have sworn that she whispered to Lawrence and that he whispered back. With even more confidence he could have sworn that a wave of furious anger swept over the face of Louis. A yard or so behind them, Verity Brown was looking in another direction; Joan Daubeney was lying flat on her back, some yards up the shore. No one but Samuel had seen the little incident which passed in a flash—so quickly and so utterly that he wondered whether he had not imagined it.

They all lay and basked in the sun and talked idly from time to time. Lawrence sat up suddenly.

"By Jove, Horder, I'd nearly forgotten," he said. "My wife wants you to dine and dance with us tomorrow night. The Carnival, you know. We'll have quite a small show up at the Château, and then it might be amusing later on to go out and see the revelry in the Old Town. All very medieval, you know."

"I'd love to, thanks awfully," said Horder.

"You'll get your formal invitation in due course," Lawrence went on. "But I mentioned it at once because it's a fancy-dress affair."

"Oh, fancy dress," he echoed, rather dolorously.

"The Carnival, I mean. It doesn't matter for the Chateau."

"Yes, but—"

"Wait a minute. The point is that Mrs. Holland is very kindly providing us with suitable attire for sallying out and joining the throng. Dominoes, don't you call them? If you asked her nicely she might make you one, too."

"I say, would you really?" He was not perhaps as enthusiastic as he should have been, for Verity and Joan by now were leaning on their elbows, and taking an interest in the discussion. Mrs. Holland, too, sat up and took notice; and especially she took notice of the expressions on the two girls' faces.

"Of course," she said. 'I've got your two done, and it won't take long to run up another. Same uniform, I suppose?"

Sam did his best to make his thanks sound cordial. He was still struggling when Kershaw suddenly appeared on the scene.

"Pardon the intrusion," he said—and once more Sam was not sure whether he used that kind of expression naturally, or as a kind of jest—"but from the description Horder gave me of your bathing parties, I thought I might find here just the thing I want after that tennis."

Louis de Vigny laughed, and produced the liquid refreshment.

"By Gad!" Kershaw continued, "I'll be as stiff as a poker to-morrow. Well, here's luck!"

He tossed off the glassful and sighed contentedly.

"That's put the last edge on my thirst," he said. "No, I'll have to go to the hotel to quench it."

For a few minutes he stood discussing the game and the last time he had played it. Lawrence de Vigny smiled as if a sudden idea had struck him.

"I say, Kershaw," he said. "You won't be too stiff to dance to-morrow, will you?" And he extended to him the same invitation as to Samuel. "And of course your friend—what's his name? yes, Burton."

Kershaw hesitated.

"Then it's a bet," Lawrence went on quickly. "My wife would be delighted, I know. Burton's an old friend of hers—they haven't met for years."

He made it sound as if he were conveying a piece of information which the other could not possibly have possessed before.

"I can't answer for Burton—" Kershaw tried to temporize.

"Oh, well, answer for yourself. And I'll get Margaret to bring her influence to bear on Mr. Burton."

Louis and the two girls looked embarrassed by the dialogue; and Lawrence's last remark had a distinctly unpleasant ring in it. Louis, trying to smooth things over, genially urged Kershaw to accept.

"Right you are. I'd love to—but I don't want to desert Burton—"

"Where is he, by the way?" Lawrence put in.

"But if he insists on wasting such a chance of seeing life, I'll *have* to," Kershaw concluded, as if he had not heard the question.

"Good," said Louis. "Eight o'clock sharp—all three of you."

"Formal invitations to follow," Lawrence added. He did not seem particularly pleased after all that his invitation had been accepted; or possibly it was that he was annoyed at the ignoring of his question.

"You don't expect me to make *three* more dresses?" Mrs. Holland asked, genuinely taken aback. "I'm not really a dressmaker or a sewing-maid." Her voice rose indignantly.

The two brothers pacified her as best they could, and Sam again tried to help by protesting that he really oughtn't to allow her—

"Why, I certainly will do one for *you,* " she said, giving him, to his consternation, an arch look. "I promised."

The situation was explained to Kershaw, who laughed and said that he thought that both he and Burton would find all the elements of fancy dress in their ordinary wardrobes; or else he'd go over to the New Town and find something. Whereupon he was given a rough description of the pattern of the costumes—black and white, was the general *motif*—which the Château party would wear.

"Easier to get through the crowds," Lawrence said, in vague explanation. Then he scrambled to his feet.

"Must be time to think of going home," he suggested. "You're lunching with us, aren't you, Horder?"

He replied that he believed he was. He must go and dress.

"Right. Sorry we can't give you a lift—but you know why. Give me a hand with the basket as far as the hotel," and he laid hold of one end, saying it was his turn to be useful, and telling Louis and the rest to go on, he would overtake them. He would not hear of Kershaw helping or would not do so until the entrance of the hotel was reached. There he left them, with a request that the basket should be put in the charge of the *concierge* "to be called for."

Sam hurried up to his room to change. He glanced out of the window and saw that though Louis and the two girls were just going out of sight, Mrs. Holland seemed to have been left behind; she was just by the entrance to the footpath. Then he saw her stop, rest one hand on the fence and with the other try, he judged, to extract a stone from her shoe. Lawrence de Vigny overtook her, and perhaps spoke to her, for Samuel saw her look up—and he found it very easy to picture her slow smile as she did so. Mrs. Holland's smiles were hard worked.

He was thoughtful when he came down. He had told the *concierge* to procure some kind of car, so he had plenty of time and decided on a few minutes' tranquillity on the veranda. Burton was there, and he and Kershaw were consuming two long drinks of a purplish hue. To his mingled surprise and annoyance they nodded to him quite distantly: and worse was to follow, for after glancing quickly in his direction, as he sat himself down a couple of tables away, they lowered their voices and conversed in what was little more than a whisper. He could not but begin to think, with a good deal of anger both at them and at his own simplicity, that Kershaw's almost effusive friendliness of the morning had been assumed for some special purpose. He seemed to hear an echo of Lawrence de Vigny's question. Where *had* Burton been all the morning? Why all the mystery about it? By Jove—the courtyard.

Well, he wasn't going to be treated anyhow by a couple of toughs from the back of beyond; and he certainly wouldn't let them see that he had noticed anything.

He got up and, as he passed the two men, "I'm on to my lunch at the Château," he said. "Have you made up your minds about the dance?"

Both men looked up, frowning.

"Burton's not much of a dancer," Kershaw began, in a friendly tone, despite the frown. "I don't think—"

"Speak for yourself, Dandy," Burton interrupted sharply. "You might tell Monsieur de Vigny *I'm* delighted to accept his invitation."

He hesitated, very slightly, before the last word. Sam wondered whether he had not been very near to using the word "challenge" instead.

"And you might add, if you will," Burton went on, "that I'll answer formally when I get the formal invitation."

"Right you are," said Sam easily. "I expect they'll ring the chapel bell when they hear the good news."

Burton glowered and opened his mouth to retort, but Kershaw got in first.

"Accept for me on the same terms," he said. "I like dancing."

Burton thought better of his intention to reprove the artist for his impertinence, and instead smiled at him quite amiably.

"Sorry," he said, "my fault,"; and re-established himself in Sam's good graces.

Burton continued to smile, not very mirthfully, after the two men were alone. Dandy Kershaw's face wore a worried look. Anyone might have supposed that it was the latter who was not much of a dancer.

CHAPTER VI

SAMUEL SKETCHES

THE *"AUTO DE LUXE"* provided by the hotel to convey Sam to his lunch had not much "luxe" in its appearance, but both it and its driver manifested plenty of "go." He had forgotten that the short cut which he and Kershaw had taken was not a practicable course for cars, because it ran through, and temporarily was swept away by the Old Town, as by a landslide. A longish detour therefore was necessary and he was grateful for the turn of speed, even though it produced a bumpy progress. In fact he felt quite exhilarated—"all this rich food. Jog up the liver a bit," he muttered to himself at the most sensational moment—and he arrived at the Château in excellent spirits. And as the lunch progressed he wondered whether a jaded liver had not been responsible for all his ideas of friction or worse amongst the party.

For nothing could have been jollier than the lunch party; there seemed to be no change in the relationships, but the spirit was one of camaraderie instead of animosity. Lawrence, for example, chaffed his wife about her rediscovery of her old flame, and mildly ragged her about the way in which she had slipped off for the morning.

"Mooning with him in the romantic alleys of the Old Town, eh, dear?"

And Margaret laughed quite girlishly, with colour in her cheeks and freely admitted that he had guessed right.

"Very good for you, Lawrence," she said. "I've spoilt you."

And Lawrence laughed in turn and said that he was making up for it by spoiling *her* now.

"I've asked your young man to dine here to-morrow night," he told her, and Samuel made bold to put in his oar and announce Mr. Burton's acceptance.

Margaret groaned in mock resignation.

"Poor Bill! He never could dance. Well, well, don't say you didn't bring it on yourself, my dear. I shall have to sit out with him—if only for the sake of the rest of my sex."

Verity and Joan protested; neither of them had seen the great Mr. Burton yet, but how could they better get to know him than by sitting out with him in some secluded and romantic nook in the Château? And this, of course, brought Louis into the picture, with Samuel lending him slightly self-conscious support. And then they began talking about Dandy Kershaw—it was Samuel who betrayed the nickname—and his tennis and whom they should get to dine, instead of just to dance, in order to "balance the numbers.' Then there was some talk about the arrangements, especially the costumes to be donned by the Château party before they started out, somewhere about half-past eleven, to frolic among the ruins.

"By the way, Lawrence," his brother asked, "have you given old Pierre Drousse permission to have his stall in the corner by the new bridge?"

Lawrence said he certainly had done so, and advised Samuel to purchase a few balloons and what not on his way up to the Château for dinner.

The conversation, in other words, was perfectly normal and dealt with the trivialities of life in an amiable way. And as the food and wine were such as only are to be found in France, the company found it easy to magnify their slightest jokes into brilliant wit: and kindliness grew as the meal progressed, and at the end of it, when admirable coffee and liqueurs had been disposed of (Samuel grew hot to think of cognac which earlier in his trip he had been imbecile enough to commend), the six easily sorted themselves into couples. That is to say Joan and Louis sauntered away, on the best of terms with one another, all thought of Mrs. Holland buried and forgotten, and Lawrence and Margaret sat on the terrace and smiled harmoniously to see the couple go. And then Verity reminded Samuel that he really ought not to waste the opportunity—he must get his sketch-book at once; and Samuel begged her to show him his way about—if Madame de Vigny really didn't mind his treating the Château like that. The de Vignys were delighted and smiled to see the second couple saunter off—in another direction. And finally Margaret de Vigny rose, announcing that she had plenty to do indoors and could not waste any more time, even on such a glorious afternoon, and as she passed her husband she stooped and kissed the top of his head. And after she had gone, Lawrence sat on, still smiling and staring into space, and then he too sauntered into the Château.

The ostensible reason why Verity had taken charge of Samuel also provided an admirable means of maintaining the state of *tête-à-tête*. It was sufficient to catch a glimpse of Joan and Louis wandering towards a tower or an enticing corner of the battlements for Verity to decide that the artistic possibilities were greater from some distant view-point. It would be misleading to suggest that she made it too plain that all this was for her own or even Samuel's sake; on the contrary it was, she explained, of Joan that she was thinking, and when she and her escort—or perhaps her convoy—finally selected their "pitch," this introduced easily enough the subject which was weighing most heavily on Samuel's mind, lightened as it had been by the geniality of lunch.

"You see," said Miss Brown, "Joan's my greatest friend, and that's made it rather awkward. She wouldn't desert me, and that meant that Louis has always had the two of us to look after. Hence your immediate success."

"Thank you," said Sam.

There was an interval during which the artist behaved as artistically as he could—much flourishing of pencil and the like. Miss Brown insisted upon inspecting the earlier pages in his sketch-book and showed sufficient familiarity with the jargon of modern art-criticism to make him feel that, when she praised, she did so with good reason.

"I say, Miss Bro—Look here, you don't mind my calling you Verity, do you?"—(he gathered that she had no rooted objection)—"I wish you'd tell me what was wrong with that remark of mine this morning. You remember—something I said about that—what's his name—Burton."

"Not very fortunate, my lad; but all's well again now, I think. Every one was a bit chippy this morning. I don't quite know why. We've all been getting on one another's nerves, I suppose. You know, the same thing: three women and only two men. And so very much a family affair—"

"I should have thought that made it easier."

"Then I should think you're a poor, lonely orphan, aren't you?"

He admitted that he was.

"And besides," she went on, "you must remember that the de Vignys aren't really English. They've been brought up in England, of course, and their tastes, anyhow on the outside, are English, but inside—well, they're relics of the old French nobility."

"Jolly hard to realize it," said Samuel. "I mean to say, Lawrence—I have to call him that, I can't go calling him Monsieur or anything—Lawrence is so very—well, quiet."

"Where have you been to? D'you really expect every Frenchman to behave like a caricature at the Holborn Empire?"

"Is he really jealous—I mean about Burton?"

"Oh, I don't suppose so. He and Margaret always seem to get along very quietly. He's very nice to her, but I shouldn't say he was wildly devoted to her. But that's where his race tells—you know, Caesar's wife and so on."

"And his ancestors enjoyed *droit de seigneur,* eh?"

"I suppose so," said Miss Brown in a tone which made it pretty plain that she really did not understand the question.

"And what about Louis?"

"He's a splendid person, isn't he?"

"Seems a jolly good sportsman. D'you think he and Joan—"

"Don't ask me. I don't think they either of them know."

"It struck me that Lawrence didn't exactly encourage the idea."

"Lawrence doesn't encourage anything much."

"And Louis is full of encouragement."

"Meaning?"

"Well, what about Mrs. Holland?"

"Isn't she *awful?*"

Samuel cordially agreed, and really believed that he had no doubts on the subject.

"As a matter of fact, it *was* rather queer this morning," Verity went on. "Lawrence and Margaret certainly had had a bit of a row—and then there was something up between Lawrence and Louis. I'm sure Louis only invited Mrs. Holland to join us just to annoy Lawrence. And he'd got some other queer idea in his head—you know, about the Renault. As near as no matter he accused Lawrence of having done in the magneto himself, on purpose."

"What on earth for?"

"That's just it. It couldn't have been to prevent Margaret meeting Mr. Burton because there was the two-seater."

There was another pause.

"Oh, I say, that's *jolly* good," cried Verity, remembering that Art, not conversation, was the main business of the afternoon. Samuel also was conscious, a little guiltily, that he had been showing a rather vulgar curiosity.

"I tell you what," he said. "I'd awfully like to try and draw that bridge—the one which goes over to the tennis-court."

They made their way along the battlements to a point beyond the chapel, whence Miss Brown thought that he might get the view he wanted. He was not, however, very enthusiastic.

"I suppose one can't get to that little island?" he said, pointing to a rocky projection from the river. Miss Brown was a little doubtful.

"You have to be jolly careful; the current is so strong," she said. "But there *is* a boat. Let's go and find out."

She led the way to the tower from which the bridge started. They crossed the bridge and Samuel exclaimed at the view from its windows. They descended to the gallery by the changing rooms, and thence to the little dock, in which a small rowing-boat was moored. It was, however, held fast by a chain, and the chain was padlocked.

"Perhaps Holland's got a key," Verity suggested.

They went into the court, and discovered the professional busily engaged in re-stringing a racquet. He used as his "workshop" the dark space to the left as you entered from the dock, underneath the end penthouse on the hazard side. He had, of course, to work by electric light, and since the "workshop" ended in a wall short even of the "grille" it was by no means spacious.

"Yes, I've got a key," Holland informed them, after greeting them with his usual dark smile. "Here it is," and he took it down from a nail on the wall. In answer to their further inquiries, he said that there was no particular difficulty about landing on the island—"the Cod's Head, it's called, or something of the kind," he told them.

They chatted for a few minutes, Samuel being interested to know what life was like for a tennis professional in a foreign country. Holland seemed satisfied enough. "I don't get a great deal of play," he admitted, "but both Mr. Louis and Mr. Lawrence are first class, so what I do get is good. And there's something of a revival in France now that the World Champion is a Frenchman."

As for life in general: "Well, there's a lot to be said for St. André," the professional said. "I'm not one of the sociable sort; and my wife—she's Australian, you know—likes it a deal better than living in a villa in a London suburb. And if we do want society— well, quite a lot of English people come to St. André, and I reckon more will come in future."

Samuel took the key, promising to hang it up on its peg again if Holland had gone before they returned. He and Verity embarked and set out for the island. Holland, they found, was right. Though the stream was strong the voyage and landing were accomplished with little difficulty. The view was all that could be desired, and Sam was soon busy transferring it to his sketch-book.[2] Verity removed shoes and stockings and dabbled her feet in the river.

"Don't fall in," Sam adjured her, laughing. "I don't guarantee a rescue in this tide."

The time passed swiftly and pleasantly, until Verity, glancing at her watch, cried out that it was high time she went back to the Château. Reluctantly—and he fancied that his companion shared his reluctance—he rowed back to the dock and made fast the boat. They looked into the tennis-court but found that Holland was not there, and that the "postern gate" was locked.

"What a bore," said Samuel. "I'll have to go right round."

"Better come and have tea at the Chateau," Verity suggested, but to this he would not assent.

"There's such a thing as outstaying your welcome," he observed.

"Oh, if you feel like *that* about it, I'll skip over and fetch the spare key and let you out."

The young man, however, had another bright idea. Could he go and make another sketch, all by himself, while tea was on? He'd like to draw that round tower—Pantaloon's Tower, or something like that, Lawrence had called it—from the far side; that is, from the kitchen-garden. Then if Verity would be an angel, and bring along the key after she'd had tea . . .? The plan was approved—' if you really don't want any tea," she said. Samuel felt that she ought to have made some polite allusion to the artistic temperament, but even his reference to his habit of forgetting time and hunger and everything when he was at work, only evoked an amused smile.

"I'll show you the way," she said, and led him across the upper gallery which, at its far end, gave upon a winding stone staircase.

"What's up above?" asked Sam.

"Just a little round room, with a couple of chairs in it. But we go down. Careful!"

The girl led the way. The staircase was at first fairly well lit, by a window, at eye-level, at the point where the gallery entered it. But a turn or so later Sam understood the reason for the warning,

[2] See Part II. No. 2.

for not only was the staircase dark but also the stairs were unexpectedly steep. He brushed up against the wall, and then encountered Miss Brown's hand, thoughtfully extended to arrest his further progress. He took it and they went on hand in hand, even past the next window; but this one was nearly at floor level, which perhaps was justification enough. And then, though the stairs became appreciably less steep, the darkness fell again.

"I'm down!" Verity exclaimed and let go of his hand. It was pitch dark. Sam could hear her rattling something, either a bolt or a key; he took two steps forward and waited.

A door swung open, inwards, and Verity stepped back, literally into his arms.

"Mind your head," said Sam, with a breathless laugh, and then they stepped out to the left into the sunlight, both of them a little red of cheek.

"It's always kept bolted on the inside," Verity informed him, as if the door was the main subject of both their thoughts, while Sam commented on the thickness of the walls. "Go ahead," she continued, with a wave of her hand. "I won't bolt you out. Go and make a pretty picture, and we'll come and see how you've got on when we've had our tea."

But fortunately (as it happened) she did not leave Sam to explore the kitchen-garden alone. As a matter of fact there was not much to explore, as is usually the way in kitchen-gardens except for those who can take a keen interest in other people's parsley and artichokes. They strolled along a gravel path beneath the windows of the "changing rooms." At the end of the building were two "doors, one evidently opening on to that staircase at the end of the far gallery which he had noticed in the morning. It was locked and bolted; and so too was the door beside it, which apparently led to a gardener's sanctum—a kind of half-basement underneath the gallery and changing rooms. They walked on, past the iron railings through which they could see the "corner" where Old Pierre Drousse would next evening be selling balloons and false noses, and along the foot of the outer wall. It was evident, since it was provided with musket slits—or at all events a more recent form of loophole than those up on the fortifications of the main Château— that this part of the Château was comparatively modern. They reached a short flight of steps leading to a little round watch-tower. Sam mounted them only to find that the watch-tower was a less admirable vantage point for his sketch than he had hoped.

There was no doubt that Pantaloon's Tower was picturesque enough, and he said as much.

"Funny they blocked up those windows," he commented, referring to two which were solidly filled in with masonry. It was perhaps an ungrateful comment, since he had to thank the masonry for Verity's helping hand. She could only tell him—as indeed he could see for himself—that it had been done many years ago.

"All the windows originally were just arrow-slits, I think," she told him, "and I suppose Lawrence's great-great-grandfather thought it would be an improvement to open them out into windows, and later on his great-grandfather decided that you could have too much of a good thing. Well, what about drawing it from here?"

Sam explained his objections, chief of which was the foreground. So firm was he that it was finally decided to collect the key of the "postern gate"; and in due course Samuel was satisfactorily established on a bank outside the walls, whilst Verity returned to tea, promising to come and see him and his sketch afterwards.

Perhaps the "artistic temperament" was less imaginary than his friends freely suggested. For though when he started his drawing[3] his thoughts dwelt more on Miss Brown than on the sketching it came as quite a shock suddenly to hear her voice calling him and to see her walk out from the door of the tennis-court. He called out in reply, shut up his book, and hastened to meet her.

He reported that he had made good progress, exhibiting his sketch.

"What time is it?" he asked, and was staggered to learn that it was nearly half-past six. They stood talking for a few minutes, by one of the projecting angles of the wall, and then moved together towards the postern gate.

Verity assured him that Margaret de Vigny wouldn't be in the least bit insulted because he didn't go up to the Château and thank her.

"As a matter of fact she's got a headache and is lying down," she told him; "I expect it's the sun."

"What rotten luck," said Sam. "I hope she'll be all right by to-morrow."

"Oh yes; I expect so."

---

[3] See Part II. No. 3. a

As he was departing, Verity told him that there would be no
bathing parade next day; "such a lot to see about before the Carnival," she explained. Sam's spirits were dashed, but rose again
when Verity agreed that that would not interfere with her own before-breakfast bathe.

"*Au revoir,* Sam," she said and locked him out. He walked
briskly down towards Holland's cottage; the small change in his
trouser pocket seemed unusually heavy and jingly, and he discovered that after all he had forgotten to hang up the boat-key as he
had promised the professional that he would do. Neither Holland
nor his wife was to be seen—the cottage seemed to be shut—so,
hoping that it would not matter, he decided to keep the key and
return it to Verity next morning.

When he got back to the hotel he was surprised to find that it
was a scene of cosmopolitan animation: no less than three parties
of visitors—all of them "foreigners," said the *concierge*—had arrived. He remembered that on his own arrival the manager had
said something about visitors for the Carnival. He inquired the
whereabouts of Messrs. Burton and Kershaw and was informed
that after lunch they had hired a car and departed on an inland excursion, and that they had said that they could not be back for dinner.

CHAPTER VII

SAMUEL TRIES IT ON

AS IS THE WAY with Englishmen in foreign countries, Samuel regarded the newcomers to the Hotel Splendide, when they appeared in their several parties for dinner, with some contempt and animosity. The fact that he had arrived two days before them gave him a proprietary feeling; they had no right to talk so loudly and to be so much at home, to know (from their guide-books) more about the Old Town and the Château than he did as the result of his visits, and to be so shamelessly ready to cross-examine the hotel staff about the forthcoming Carnival.

However, by dint of sitting quietly on the veranda, he managed to learn quite a lot from their conversation. The Carnival, it seemed, might truly be said to rank with the Palio at Siena or the Gipsies' Pilgrimage to Les Saintes Maries as a survival of the Middle Ages, and it was still unspoilt by Tourist Agencies.

The conversation got on his nerves. He had come to regard St. André-sur-Mer as a silent, deserted spot; these English and American voices shattered his illusion. Disgruntled, he retired early to bed, only to find that he could still hear not only the hum of voices but most of the talk itself. To-night sleep did not come to him easily; he lay awake and stared through his balcony windows at the stars. Gradually the conversation below died away, and the scrape of chairs told of the guests' departure bed-wards.

"That's better," thought Sam and rejoiced in the silence. He dozed gently, only to be woken a short while later by the arrival of a car. What a row the engine made! He swore, for he felt so wide-awake that he doubted whether he would go to sleep at all. In desperation he got out of bed, wrapped himself in his dressing-gown, lit a cigarette, and strolled out on to his balcony. The car departed with many "Good nights" and "Thank you's"; peace descended again on the still night.

Had the car brought yet more visitors? Or was it Burton and Kershaw back at last? Samuel, with fresh annoyance, heard voices again on the veranda; it did not lessen his annoyance that they

were lowered so discreetly that he could neither recognize them
nor distinguish one word from another. He finished his cigarette
and went back to bed, and found that his brief excursion had all
the effects of a narcotic.

He woke again, with a sudden and horrible jar, and wondered
what he had been dreaming. Burton—that was it, Burton had been
shouting—"I tell you she's miserable. And by God, if I meet
that—Frenchman alone . . ." Had he dreamt it? Or had he really
heard the shout? He lay and listened intently, his heart beating
fast. All he could hear was the faint murmurs of a single voice.
Was the picture which he conjured up the true one? Of Burton losing his self-control, and Kershaw firmly but quietly shutting him
up and talking, on and on, to pacify and calm him? If only he
could hear . . . but the narcotic of the night air was working
strongly in him; he did not even know when the two men left the
veranda.

Next morning started uneventfully. True, the bathe with Verity
was an event every time it happened, but there was again no "rescue from drowning"; and there was a flavour of monotony in
Sam's failure once more to return the boat-key, which he found
lying reproachfully on his dressing-table when he got back from
his bathe.

Burton and Kershaw smiled a welcome to him at breakfast, and
afterwards the three men talked awhile. They were going in to St.
André—the New Town—and offered Sam a lift; he thanked them,
but declined. He meant to spend the morning with his sketch-book
in the Old Town. However, they agreed that they would all go up
to the Château together to dine and Kershaw undertook to order a
car.

They departed. Sam, sitting on the veranda, narrowly escaped
falling a victim to one of the new arrivals; he looked up from his
paper just in time to recognize the gleam in the eye of a determined spinster, who, guide-book in hand, was staring at him from
a neighbouring chair. He fled to his room for his sketch-book.

And then he paused. He had suddenly remembered the costume
which Mrs. Holland was making for him. Or was that just a joke?
What ought he to do about it? Perhaps, though the party at the
Château were too busy, she would be taking her usual morning
bathe, and he could meet her more or less accidentally . . . Quite
indignantly he assured himself that he had not altered the opinion
which he had expressed to Verity. She was pretty awful; but then
he must do something about that fancy dress, he supposed.

He was so uncertain whether the business about the dress had been seriously meant or not that he had not the face to go up to the cottage on purpose to inquire; so he ensconced himself on his balcony and waited. The time slipped by, and the prospects of his sketching grew more and more remote. It must have been nearly half-past eleven before a figure suddenly appeared from the path by the cottage and walked across to the shore. Samuel recognized Mrs. Holland.

He went downstairs and sauntered out of the hotel and along the shore. The new-comers seemed divided in their views as to whether the sea or the sights was the proper occupation at St. André; one party had decided for the former, the others were nowhere to be seen and so presumably had chosen the latter.

Mrs. Holland was sitting on the hot sand. She observed Samuel's approach and greeted him with a smile, a shade less friendly perhaps than those which previously she had bestowed on him.

"Good morning," she said. "Aren't you bathing this morning either? Rather a pity to waste such a lovely day."

Samuel noticed that from time to time Mrs. Holland pronounced her "r's" like "w's"; he fancied that she thought it lent charm to her words.

He smiled and said that if he did too much bathing he couldn't keep his eyes open after dinner and if he was to dance to-night—

"I thought perhaps you didn't care to bathe alone," she answered.

"Oh, I dare say that's partly why, too," he confessed. "If I'd known you were going to bathe, though—"

"Go on," she said, evidently pleased. "And really I oughtn't to be bathing, you know. There's that fancy dress of yours."

"Oh I say, are you really making one for me? I wasn't sure whether you meant it."

"Of course I did. And if you'll wait a few minutes, I'll try it on you. It's meant to be worn over your clothes, you know," she added dryly, as she noticed his embarrassed look.

With that she rose to her feet, slipped off her wrap and elaborately stretched herself. She glanced at Samuel from beneath lowered eyelids, to see whether he was duly watching her, and her lips curved into her slow smile.

"I'll make it a quick one," she said, and ran down to the sea.

While he sat and waited, Sam decided that really she wasn't a bad sort—a bit common, perhaps, or it might simply be that her Australian accent suggested the Cockney. He had better wait till she had finished her bathe and discover when the ceremony of "trying it on" was to take place.

She was as good as her word; a quick swim, and she ran back to her wrap. She did not put it on, however, but flung herself full length on the sand beside the artist.

"Five minutes of this sun and I'll be dry," she said, "and then you can come straight along to the cottage to be tried on. Got a cigarette?"

She smoked it in silence, then sat up, flung her wrap carelessly round her like a cloak and bade Samuel come along to the cottage. At the door she stopped him.

"Such a mess inside," she said. "I'll bring the dress out into the garden."

As she returned, carrying a black and white garment on her arm, she pulled off her rubber bathing cap and shook her hair loose. She tossed the check dress to Samuel and told him to put it on, and while he did so she gave herself a perfunctory sort of rub down with her bathing wrap and then discarded it.

Samuel struggled into the costume. It was not at all his idea of a domino; rather it was a pierrot's dress, all black and white checks—something like a boiler suit, the ankles and wrists drawn in with elastic bands and the trouser portion more elegant and baggy. He found it quite a job, having got his feet through the trousers, to get the coat part over his shoulders.

Mrs. Holland laughed, and it did not lessen Samuel's embarrassment when he observed that in the rubbing-down process one of her shoulder-straps had gone sadly astray, and when next moment she came and assisted him.

"How's the belt?" she said, having approved the "set" of the shoulders, and she encircled his waist with two strong brown arms.

"Capital," said Samuel, hastily.

"That'll do," she answered, giving him a slight squeeze, and leaving him uncertain whether or not she had misapplied his remark.

However, nothing worse followed. She helped him doff the garment again, and assured him that it fitted quite as well as the others which she had made, and suggested that he might take it with him then and there.

"I say—what about paying for it?" he asked awkwardly.

"Oh, Mr. de Vigny bought yards of the stuff," she said.

"Yes, but—" he went on, in embarrassment, "I mean you, and all the work—"

Mrs. Holland sniffed.

"I told you before—I'm not a sewing maid. Just because Len and I aren't asked to dinner—"

Samuel apologized abjectly.

"That's all right. You're a nice boy," Mrs. Holland relented. "And if you want to pay me for it—not that I want it, mind you—what d'you say to drawing my portrait?"

"A poor reward," said Sam. "I'm no good at portraits."

"I'm sure you are. Anyhow—that's my terms. Oh, and you might save me a walk, if you took charge of the other two dresses. I've got 'em all done up ready. You're dining at the Château, aren't you?"

And so Samuel returned to the hotel rather early for lunch, and bore with him two brown paper parcels and one self-evident fancy dress whose presence on his arm brought him into fresh and instant peril of acquaintance with four Americans resting in the lounge after their visit to the Old Town.

After lunch he was again hard put to it to escape; he sacrificed his coffee to his determination to avoid fresh acquaintance and set out for the Old Town. There at least he could count on a measure of solitude, and if the event proved that the measure was not great and he had little chance to do more than sketch a corner here or a fragment there,[4] still he managed to learn his way about a little, and even to mark down one or two alluring spots for future sketching; needless to say, his programme contemplated the companionship of Verity Brown.

He came back to the hotel in good time; he was quite excited at the prospect of the dinner and the dance and somehow felt that he was responsible for getting Burton and Kershaw there at the proper moment.

Consequently he was rather annoyed and fussed to find that they had not yet returned. However, whilst he was on his balcony—his evening clothes all laid out ready in the room behind him—he heard and then saw them. He leant over and called to them not to be late.

"Late!" Burton echoed in surprise. "But we're not dining till eight, are we?"

"Yes, but—"

"Keep calm, young man," Kershaw put in. "There's plenty of time—unless you don't want to go by car but on foot after all."

---

[4] See Part II. No. 4.

Samuel withdrew in some disorder; he could not but recognize that he had been rather unreasonable. He consumed his soul in patience as long as he could, pottering about and making a parcel of his fancy dress; the invaluable *concierge* had produced brown paper for the purpose.

At last the time had come to change. He proceeded still with determined deliberation. He shaved with exaggerated care. He brushed and re-brushed his hair until its most rebellious plume was reduced to utter subjection. He was not satisfied with his first effort to tie his white tie in a perfect bow; he pulled it off and—Good heavens, could that be the car? By Jove, it was—and he was late after all. Fool! That tie had been quite good enough.

Needless to say the second tie was a horrible failure. And he had only one more clean one. What on earth would he do if—? Thank heavens, it was a success.

He heard Kershaw calling him from the road. He went to the balcony—though he was careful to keep out of sight—and shouted back, "Just coming. What's the hurry?" and felt rather pleased with himself. He hurried into coat and waistcoat, equipped himself with watch and cigarettes and match-case, remembered his pocket-book (By Jove, though, he had done nothing about balloons and false noses. Well, he'd have to do that after dinner somehow—that stall which was to be by the bridge). He gave a last glance at the mirror and observed with annoyance that his hair was again in open revolt; but there was no time for that now. He hurried downstairs, complete with parcels, and found Burton and Kershaw, anything but impatient, consuming cocktails in the lounge.

"Have one?" the former invited him. He declined, rather stiffly; for though Kershaw was as usual living up to his nickname, his companion apparently had thought a dinner-jacket and black tie formal enough for the occasion.

Perhaps Burton guessed his thoughts, for he laughed, rather harshly, and said, "Another bird of paradise. Sorry to disgrace you both. But I never reckoned on striking High Life down here."

"Oughtn't we to start?" Sam asked, feeling very tactful.

"Right you are," Kershaw answered, and finished his cocktail at a gulp. The three got into their car, the *concierge* holding the door open for them and bowing deeply. Their departure caused quite a flutter on the veranda.

Kershaw talked fast and lightly during the drive; he received little support, for Samuel was preoccupied in pleasurable excitement and Burton was gloomy and frowning.

Here they were, at the main gate already. How awful! Were they too early? Here they were at the Château itself. The butler, however, did not seem surprised at their arrival—or even at Samuel's three paper parcels. Indeed, he did not ask what they were, but allowed Sam to deposit them in a corner of his own choosing.

"They'll be wanted later," he said by way of general explanation alike to the two friends and to the butler, who might or might not speak English. They were ushered with some pomp into the inner hall; Samuel distinctly heard Burton swear softly and was himself rather taken aback to see that the company was large— perhaps twenty people, including themselves. Margaret and Lawrence de Vigny were welcoming them—Sam was being introduced right and left and was bowing and murmuring nothing in particular in a singular mixture of French and English—until at last he found himself on safe ground talking to Verity Brown.

"I say, I never expected this," he said. "Thought it would be quite a small affair—for dinner, anyhow."

"It's all right," she smiled at him. "You're sitting next to me, with an American girl—married to a Frenchman—the other side of you. She's not here yet."

He heaved a sigh of relief, and looked round to see how his two companions were getting on. In his confusion he had failed to observe Burton's meeting with his hostess, but he saw that he was now talking easily to her, perhaps apologizing for his sombre attire. Kershaw was one of a group which included Joan and Louis, and apparently was still at the top of his form. Two more couples arrived, and fresh introductions were effected; Samuel gathered that one of the new arrivals was the lady by whom he was to sit, but before he could clear this up, dinner was announced and Lawrence de Vigny proclaimed that the proceedings were informal— would they all kindly look for their places—and not be insulted if they were not all in the seats of the mighty.

They moved into the dining-room and Samuel soon found himself in animated conversation with the vivacious American whom he had just met. He sipped a glass of incomparable sherry and let his gaze wander round the table. Joan and Louis were side by side, nearly opposite to him. Kershaw he could not see—he must be on the same side of the table as himself. Lawrence, of course, was at one end of the long table, talking to a lady who looked singularly like the traditional "vamp." At the other end sat Margaret, with Burton next her on her left.

CHAPTER VIII

THE DANCE OF DEATH

THE DINNER was so cheerful that it might, not unjustly, have been called boisterous. Samuel noticed only one exception; whenever he glanced along towards his hostess, he saw that beside her Burton still wore his aspect of frowning gloom.

He made some inquiries, of his two neighbours, about the evening's programme. The idea, he learnt, was that they should dance till half-past eleven or so and then (reversing the traditional procedure) assume fancy dresses and masks; those, that is, who proposed to take the Carnival seriously.

"Quaint idea, isn't it?" the American lady laughed. "To bring a change of clothes with you when you go out to dine."

Verity confirmed the statement that they were all to change at the Château.

"Easy enough for you men," she said. "The word went round about the sort of uniform you're to wear—some kind of dominoes, I mean, not necessarily black and white. That's just for us. But some of the women—well, I should say they'd much rather have dressed up in front of their own dressing-tables."

"It'll take an awful time, won't it?"

Verity giggled.

"Not for all of us. Strictly between you and me, Sam, I've not got *much* on now; and I shall have even less when I'm in my fancy dress."

At the end of the table Lawrence de Vigny rose to his feet—a shade unsteadily, perhaps—and called for silence.

"*Mesdames et Messieurs,*" he began and proceeded, alternately in French and English to explain the proceedings. "And we shall," he concluded, "abandon for once the admirable English custom of the men staying behind after dinner. The English protocol," he added, "is the most important contribution of Great Britain to civilization; but it demands port—whereas champagne demands brandy."

They trooped out into a room which Samuel had not seen before—a great hall, perhaps the real banqueting hall, with a minstrels' gallery in which a dance orchestra was already ensconced. The orchestra struck up a lively measure and in a twinkling every one was dancing—no, not every one: Burton was engaged in a laborious conversation with a skittish young thing in a long silvery frock, who looked anything but pleased to find herself a sort of wall-flower.

Samuel took no account of time; he danced with vigour and without interruption, save for an occasional visit to the buffet, established in the dining-room with remarkable celerity. Burton seemed to be one of its most regular occupants, and Kershaw also was a frequent visitor. Sam spoke to each of them once or twice, and noticed that whether or not their potations were many or deep they were little affected. Burton remained sullen, and Kershaw hilarious; but both seemed steadier of foot and tongue than the young artist, despite what he considered to be his moderation. One or two more parties arrived, including two or three unattached men, so that the non-dancer Burton no longer had to inflict his immobility on a reluctant partner.

It must have been half-past eleven or even later, when a couple arrived in fancy dress. Lawrence de Vigny met them and firmly escorted them to the buffet, bidding them on no account venture out till the rest of the party were similarly attired. Then he hurried away to reappear next moment in the Minstrels' Gallery. The orchestra played a long chord, then was silent; Lawrence announced that the time had come to mask for the Carnival. With laughter and shouts they all moved to the inner hall, where the butler directed the men to the smoking-room whilst a number of maid-servants, picturesquely dressed in the "national" costume, took charge of the ladies. Sam was one of the last to leave the ball-room; he found Verity at his side.

"Hurry up," she said, "and meet me in the outer hall. It won't take me a minute to dress."

He nodded and she slipped away through the crowd. As he followed her he passed close to Margaret de Vigny, who had paused for a moment in the doorway. She was speaking to Burton.

"Cheer up, Billie," he heard her say. He could not catch the answer, given in a fierce, almost passionate whisper.

"Hush!" said Margaret, and then whispered too.

Burton's expression lightened and he nodded quickly once or twice. Samuel saw him disappear in the direction of the buffet.

In the inner hall he found Lawrence de Vigny talking quite ferociously to the butler. It must be confessed that the artist was in no state to follow a rapid conversation in the French tongue, but he contrived to detect that the object of Lawrence's harangue was his fancy dress.

"Oh, I say, I've got it," he said; "I'm awfully sorry. I thought you knew," and in a few words he explained how Mrs. Holland had come to entrust the parcels to him.

"Oh, good. All is well, then. Where are they?" Lawrence's good-humour instantly returned.

Samuel hastened to fetch his parcels from the outer hall. They looked rather alike, but his own was noticeably less tidy than the other two. He found the one marked "L. de V." and thrust it into his host's arms; and the latter, with a nod of thanks and a reference to his own need to hurry, in case more guests arrived, ran upstairs.

Observing Louis advancing on the butler, doubtless to repeat his brother's inquiries, Sam went to meet him and delivered the second parcel. Louis, too, hurried upstairs and Samuel found himself alone in the hall, save for the butler. The latter waved him towards the smoking-room, but instead with an elaborate explanation which bewildered but silenced the butler he finally retired to the outer hall. (After all, he was going to put more on, not take things off; it really didn't matter if more guests arrived and found him.)

He tore open his parcel, crumpled up the paper, and started to don his black and white costume. It was not as easy as he expected—he had forgotten that Mrs. Holland had helped him into it before—and he had barely finished when Verity appeared. A Pierrette, but of a Modernist School: black and silver shoes, a skirt (if it could be so called) of jagged stripes of black and silver, and a bodice which surely must be as metallic as it looked, since apparently it required no shoulder-straps for its support.

"I say," Samuel exclaimed, "is—is that all you're wearing?"

"Don't say you're shocked. Don't you like it? Good heavens, it's much more than I wear when I'm bathing."

"Yes, but—" he began: he really was rather shocked.

"Poor old thing," said Miss Brown sadly. "You'll get over it when you grow up. Now come on; we'll go and hide in the gallery by the tennis-court until the dancing's started again and then we can come back and dance together—oh, several times—because no one will know us in our masks."

"D'you mean it?" Sam's feelings recovered rapidly.

"Well, I—rather like dancing with you."

"Do you really?" He stepped quickly towards her.

"Yes, you dance quite nicely. Got your mask?"

"Good Lord!—I never thought—"

"But surely Mrs. Holland—"

"No, she never said anything about it."

In considerable perturbation he thrust his hands into the pockets of his dress: his face brightened.

"Here it is, by Jove!" he cried, and drew out a black silk mask.

"*Come* on, then," and Verity caught his hand and hurried with him to the flying bridge. They sped over it towards the light at its far ends and paused in the upper gallery on the other side.

"Where now?" Samuel asked. He felt something more than exhilarated; rather, indeed, as if he was moving hand-in-hand with a fairy along a shaft of moonlight. "The room at the top of the Tower?"

"Such hard chairs," sighed Verity.

"I know," said Sam. "The sofa," and led the way down to the lower gallery.

There are occasions when one sofa is infinitely to be preferred to two chairs, hard or soft; and though the upper gallery was lit by a soft ceiling light, the lower gallery was comparatively dark. The sofa was by the tall windows; the moonlight had to dodge the shadows of the Château and the lead frames of the diamond panes of glass before it could find its way in; and altogether the two black and white figures provided an admirable illustration of the value of protective colouring. All this no doubt had its share of responsibility; and something must be laid to the account of champagne, and to Sam's gallantry as a life saver, and to youth. In other words, Samuel Horder and Verity Brown kissed with all the fervour of film stars.

Kisses and conversation are mutually destructive; little had been said when there came the sound of footsteps on the bridge. The young couple shrunk hastily apart—a needless precaution, for they were barely visible from the upper gallery.

"Margaret, my dear, I can't stand it."

"Yes, you can, Billie. You must. It's your own fault. No, don't stop to argue here. There's a little room where we can talk. No one will come up there. But only for a few minutes. Then I must go back."

Breathlessly, Sam and Verity watched Margaret de Vigny, closely followed by Burton, cross the upper gallery. The latter still wore his dinner-jacket; the former a more restrained version of Verity's dress.

"Wait, I'll put on the light," they heard Margaret say. "It's up here. Mind your head."

They disappeared from view.

"What—what—" Samuel stuttered.

"*Hush!*" said Verity, quite fiercely. "Oh, I was afraid—poor old Margaret."

"D'you mean that she—that she and Burton—"

"Yes," Verity answered, softly. "I'm afraid so. Joan told me something. She was only a kid when Margaret married Lawrence, but—"

Samuel decided that it was absurd to waste time in so unprofitable, not to say depressing, a conversation.

"But you and I, Verity," he began, and tried gently to draw her towards him.

"Don't, Sam," she said. "It's rather—horrid, isn't it?"

Before he could reply, more footsteps sounded from the bridge. This time, a solitary figure appeared; a man, masked and wearing a black and white costume identical with Sam's. Without pause or hesitation he crossed the gallery and in turn entered the Tower of Pantaloon.

"Gosh!" said Samuel. "Who's that?"

"Either Lawrence or Louis," Verity's voice was quite husky. 'If it's Lawrence and he finds them—Listen."

They sat in strained silence. There came a heavyish clanging sound. Verity drew a deep breath of relief.

"He's gone into the kitchen-garden," she said.

"Yes, but he'll see the light," Sam suggested nervously. "Hadn't we—or you—better tell them?"

"Yes. All right. I'll call Margaret down," said Verity, and ran quickly up the steps to the upper gallery. At the top she paused irresolutely.

"Hullo, is that you, Joan?" she called to someone on the bridge.

"Yes. Where's Louis?"

Joan Daubeney, dressed exactly like Verity, joined her on the gallery. Sam watched the two girls intently; they were like two fantastic toys in a magical toy-shop.

"Oh, was it Louis who came along a minute ago?"

"Yes."

There was no mistaking the meaning of the hard note in Joan's voice; one fist, too, was tightly clenched as if in anger.

"I—I expect he's waiting for you in the garden, dear," Verity said, with an effort at frivolity which failed to conceal both her surprise and her nervousness.

"Me!" was all the answer Joan gave; she darted past her into Pantaloon's Tower. Verity again hesitated.

"Sam," she called, in a low voice. "Joan says it was Louis. So I needn't—"

"Hullo, hullo, hullo!" a voice boomed loudly down the bridge. "So there's one of 'em. Where are all the rest?"

"Damn!" said Samuel, recognizing Kershaw's voice.

"Where's our wandering Sam to-night?" went on Kershaw, evidently advancing over the bridge. Afterwards Sam believed that whilst Kershaw spoke he heard a faint, muffled sound—something between a slap and the pop of a cork leaving the neck of a bottle.

"Verity," he called. "Quick. Come and hide."

But as the words left his mouth he stiffened and half rose from the sofa.

"What's that?" Verity cried, in alarm, and simultaneously Kershaw hurried up.

The noise, though muffled, as if it came from a distance, sounded like a scream.

"What's that?" asked Kershaw.

"A scream, it sounded like," Verity answered. Sam was listening intently.

"Carnival, I expect," Kershaw suggested, and for a second Samuel, in his dark retreat, accepted the theory with relief.

"No, but—" Verity began, and stopped abruptly.

The noise was repeated, and a second later was followed by a scuffling noise from Pantaloon's Tower.

"Stay there, Miss Brown," said Kershaw sharply, his heartiness suddenly gone. "I'll go and see."

Verity ran down the steps; Sam had sprung to his feet. She ran to him and he flung his arm round her and held her close.

"Oh, Sam," she whispered, shaking. "D'you think it was Lawrence after all?"

Sam held her more tightly but said nothing; his eyes and ears were occupied with the scene on the upper gallery. Kershaw had hurried across to the entrance to the Tower, and there he had met Burton, just descended from the room above. Margaret de Vigny, very white, was just behind him.

"What is it?" Kershaw asked.

"In the garden. Miss Daubeney. Someone hurt." Burton answered jerkily.

The two men conferred in whispers; then:

"Wait here, Margaret.' Burton turned to the woman. "Dandy and I will go and investigate. Don't go—and don't let anyone else come or go."

"Go and look after Margaret," Sam said to Verity. He was surprised at the huskiness of his voice, for he felt, all of a sudden, very calm and sure of himself. "Go on," he repeated, giving her a little push. She ran up and joined Margaret de Vigny by the entrance to the Tower.

It was suddenly borne in on Sam that he had been occupying a key position. He had no idea what had happened, but Burton had been wise in the orders which he had given to Margaret.

"Madame de Vigny," he called.

She started, and he heard Verity reassure her by telling her who had called. "Where do the lights turn on?"

"Up here," she answered, her voice quivering with some emotion—suspense or excitement—"Wait."

The lower gallery was suddenly flooded with light.

Sam quickly tried the door of each of the changing rooms. Each was locked and the key was on his side of the door. He ran down the far steps to the door which led to the garden—the door which he had marked as in little use. It was locked on the inside, and heavily bolted—he came back to his sofa and paused in thought. If his recollection of the geography was right, no one could get in or out of the kitchen-garden except through Pantaloon's Tower. He joined the two frightened women on the upper gallery.

"I'll go too—" he began.

"No, no," Verity begged him.

Sounds came from the stairs in the tower—a man's voice, and scuffling feet, and a sobbing noise. Joan Daubeney, half supported by Burton, came into view. She was sobbing violently, almost hysterically. She gave a cry and flung herself into Margaret's arms.

Margaret looked at Burton in silent, fearful inquiry.

"It's Louis," he said almost emotionlessly. "He's been—shot."

There was a pause of a second or two, but it seemed an age. Her wide eyes asked a further question.

"Yes, he's dead," said Burton, very gravely.

CHAPTER IX

THE EMPTY GARDEN

THERE WAS A SILENCE—how long it lasted Samuel hardly knew; he became aware that he was clutching Verity's hand very tightly, as much to keep up his own spirits as hers. Then, all of a sudden, it seemed, Dandy Kershaw was back again. The discovery had changed him, as it had changed Burton; the holiday-maker, in his case, had gone, and the hunter, the man accustomed to sudden death, had taken his place.

"This is a bad business," he said. His tone was curt, almost savage; it had something of the effect of a douche of cold water upon the group. Joan, even, ceased her sobbing, and with the rest stared at Kershaw open-eyed—in Sam's case open-mouthed too. He seemed definitely to take control of the situation.

"The poor fellow's been shot. Shot, what's more, with a small-bore rifle, if I'm not mistaken. That means—may mean—someone in the garden. We've got to make sure. No,"—he added sharply, as Burton half-turned, as if to make for the turret-stair, "if there's someone there he can't very well get away. First of all—we must tell Monsieur de Vigny."

There was another silence. Margaret gave her head a little jerk and began gently to loosen Joan's clasp. Kershaw shook his head a little doubtfully.

"I—I'll tell him," Verity half whispered, a little choke in her voice.

"Good," said Kershaw.

Samuel gave her hand a little farewell squeeze, and she turned and ran across the bridge. Burton, as if unconscious of what he was doing, started to follow her, slowly. Kershaw was deep in thought, his forehead creased in a frown and the twinkling wrinkles round his eyes all vanished, and at first did not notice, then he called to him sharply and he stopped short. As he turned, something which he could see from the bridge caught his eye. He pointed.

"Someone down there," he said.

In a flash Kershaw was at his side.

"In the tennis-court," he said. "How d'you get to it?"

"Down these stairs," Samuel answered, with a promptitude which surprised himself. "It's the only way, from this side. I'll go and see."

"You mean you can't get into it from the garden?"

"Yes."

Samuel felt that his offer was positively heroic but Kershaw, who perhaps had seen in a flash that since whoever was in the tennis court could not have just arrived there from the garden, took his offer as a matter of course. Sam ran down, round the dock and through the door to the court; it was half open and it was clearly the light streaming from it which had attracted Burton's notice. On his left, as he entered, was Holland, in what might be called his workshop. He was seated, stooping over a table: by the light of an electric lamp he was once more engaged in stringing a racquet. He was wearing old grey flannel trousers and a well-worn brown pullover—so unlike his dapper figure when he played tennis that at first Samuel hardly recognized him.

He looked up, startled, as Samuel entered, and stared blankly at him. Obviously he did not at first recognize him; then he laughed.

"Why it's Mr.—er—Horder," he said. As he detected the excitement and alarm in Sam's face, his smile faded. "What's up?" he asked.

"Accident in the garden. Mr. Louis shot!" Sam blurted out.

"Mr. Louis—shot—Good God!" There was no mistaking the shock which the news gave to the professional. He sprang up, still holding the half-strung racquet, and stared dumbly at the incongruous figure in the black and white checks.

"Better come," said Sam; then, as a happy afterthought: "Is the other door into the court locked—the one from your cottage, I mean?"

Holland nodded and followed Sam in his rapid progress back to the upper gallery. He was somewhat taken aback to find the other three there, and made an effort to murmur something sympathetic to Madame de Vigny. At that moment Verity reappeared, panting.

"Lawrence—just coming—" she gasped. "And two of the men. He's sending every one away. Telling them Louis's been taken ill. They're telephoning to the doctor—and the police."

"Good," said Kershaw. He seemed by now to have formed a plan of operations. As the first of the two footmen appeared he ordered him to stay in the gallery; the man merely looked blank.

"No one can get into the Château from the garden any other way," he said in general explanation. Then, to the three women: "You must stay too, I'm afraid. Better wait down there," and he nodded towards the sofa in the lower gallery on which Verity and Sam had been so happily seated—how short a time before! "Billie, stay with them," he added. Burton made a gesture as of protest. "Stay please," Kershaw repeated, more sharply than ever; Burton shrugged his shoulders, as if bewildered, but made no further sign of dissent.

"Horder and Holland and you," (this to the second of the footmen) "see if there's anyone in the garden. Don't touch the body, or go near it till I come."

They moved to obey his orders, with one exception. "Oh, Miss Brown," he went on, "d'you speak French? Good. Please tell this man" (he nodded at the first footman who, unlike the other, evidently knew no English and had not in the least grasped the *rôle* allotted to him) "to stay here—and when Monsieur de Vigny comes, he's to tell him—or you can if you like—to come out at once. You understand? We're none of us to go back over the bridge—till the police come."

"But—but—" she stammered.

"Understand?" he repeated. She nodded.

"Right." And he turned and disappeared down the turret stair.

The moon was bright, and the kitchen-garden almost as easily surveyed as if it had been noon. The tongue of yellow light which streamed from the open door at the foot of Pantaloon's Tower seemed to point straight to the huddle of black and white which lay, in shadow but clearly visible, at the apex of the projecting angle of wall opposite the Tower. It was with a conscious effort that they tore their eyes and their attention away and obedient to Kershaw's directions began a search of the garden. They were not, perhaps, free from some trepidation; Sam at all events felt decidedly nervous at the prospect of encountering a murderer armed with a rifle. Of the three searchers, Holland alone, with his half-strung racquet, had even the feeblest kind of weapon. Kershaw, of course, would think nothing of it, Sam said to himself, rather angrily.

The garden was not very large; the opportunities for concealment were few. It was chiefly a matter of making sure that the doors to the "gardener's shed" underneath the changing rooms were fast shut—as certainly they were; they were bolted on the outside, which disposed of the possibility of anyone being hidden inside and that no one was in the watch-tower on the wall, or concealed in one of the angles.

As Sam with Holland and the footman passed the iron railings by the "new bridge" (Kershaw was over by the body), they were startled to hear a voice. An old man with a long grey beard was standing just outside, grasping the bars rather like a monkey at the Zoo. He seemed somewhat excited, and poured out a flood of French which went a good deal too fast for the artist.

"What's he say?" he asked Holland in a low voice.

"Well—I think he wants to know—talks so fast," the professional replied, unhelpfully.

"Has he seen anyone in the garden—no, anyone get out of the garden?" Sam demanded of the footman, loudly: thus, he hoped, making the meaning plain. The man apparently understood, and interrupted the flow from beyond the bars.

"He see man—black and white—then *une dame* and then anozzer two men. They go away into Tour Panteleon. Then we come. No one other—he demands—"

"Tell him to stay where he is. When Monsieur de Vigny comes he'll talk to him."

The three continued their tour. They found no one. They came to the angle where the dead man lay. They found Kershaw and Lawrence, the latter on one knee beside the body, talking in low tones. Louis de Vigny lay in a rather huddled attitude close to the fire-step. A dark pool was slowly spreading round his head; already it had half engulfed the black mask which evidently had been torn aside by one of the earlier arrivals on the scene.

"Well?" Kershaw demanded of Samuel.

"No one—that side," the latter reported. "But there's a man by the railings there."

"What man?"

"The old fellow that sells balloons," Holland put in. "He's seen something or other."

Lawrence de Vigny looked up sharply; in the bright moonlight Sam saw him moisten his lips with his tongue, but before he could speak Kershaw curtly told the others to finish their search.

They found no trace of any human being until they reached the tower again; they were somewhat startled by a man who suddenly stepped out from the arched doorway, but it was only another man-servant—the butler, this time.

"Ou est Monsieur?" he asked.

Samuel pointed to the spot where Lawrence was; now standing and conversing earnestly with Kershaw. The butler strode in that direction and the three followed.

"No one," Sam reported; the butler poured out a flood of French even faster than that of the monkey man at the railings.

"What's it all about?" Kershaw demanded, when the recital was at an end.

"This damned Carnival," said Lawrence. "Can't get the doctor on the telephone—or the police—or only a wretched gendarme who says he can't leave the station."

There was a silence.

"That's the very limit," Kershaw said at length. "Well, we must do the best we can without them. I'm afraid the doctor couldn't help anyhow. We'd—better leave the body where it is. We've mucked up the ground pretty thoroughly—though it's too hard to show footprints anyhow, I should say."

Again he paused.

"D'you think anyone could have got over the wall?" he asked Lawrence.

"No. Not without a rope," was the answer. "And it's all soft sand at the foot of the wall—so there'd pretty certainly be traces."

"The old man by the railings?" Sam suggested.

"That's an idea," said Kershaw. "Come on, Monsieur de Vigny. Wait here, the rest of you. Don't touch anything."

In silence, broken only by respectful but horrified whispers exchanged between the men-servants, they waited while Kershaw and Lawrence hastened to the far end of the garden. The indistinct sounds of an excited conversation came to their ears. Then the two hurried back. This time it was Lawrence who issued the orders, but Samuel conjectured, rightly enough, that he had been prompted by the little man at his side.

The footman was told to betake himself to the watch-tower; the butler to station himself at the door of Pantaloon's Tower; both were to shout if they saw anything unusual or suspicious.

"We can't do any more here at the moment," Lawrence concluded. "We'll go back to the gallery and—hold a council."

The group on which they looked down from the upper gallery would, in other circumstances, have been grotesque enough: the grim standing figure in dinner-jacket, and in contrast, the three

pierrettes on the sofa—the pierrettes' expressions so out of keeping with their Carnival attire. Sam vaguely recalled a "costume"
picture—doubtless the grand success of a Victorian Academy—of
a young man, sitting in a room littered with playing cards, the can-
dles still burning and daylight creeping stealthily in between the
heavy curtains.

Lawrence led the way down the steps. The five men grouped
themselves in a semi-circle in front of the sofa.

"Now, Kershaw," Lawrence began.

"I can't say much," said Kershaw. "I was a latecomer on the
scene. The last, in fact."

"No, Holland," said Samuel.

"Ah yes, of course," Kershaw agreed. "It's like this," he addressed Lawrence. "There's only one way into the kitchen-garden
from the Château, isn't there? And we know from that old man by
the railings that pretty certainly no one came in any other way—
even if it's possible. It's quite certain no one came through the
gate in the railings."

Lawrence agreed, though still mystified about the purpose of
this preface.

"That means," Kershaw continued, "that Horder and Miss
Brown, who were sitting here, saw every one who went into the
Tower. You didn't see Holland, did you?" he ended abruptly with
the question.

"No," said Sam.

"I was stringing this racquet in the court when Mr. Horder
came in," said the professional. "First I saw or heard of it all."

"How long had you been there?"

"Oh, since about half-past eleven."

"Bit late to string racquets?" Kershaw suggested.

Holland smiled.

"No use trying to sleep with the racket they're making with the
Carnival," he answered. "There was the job to be done and," (he
sounded almost sly) "I reckoned no one would want a game before
lunch to-morrow."

Kershaw still looked rather incredulous. Holland was looking
intently at his employer, and the latter was evidently impelled by
the gaze to come to his support.

"Matter of fact Holland said something to me this morning
about working late up here," he said.

"Oh," said Kershaw, and then: "Anyhow it isn't very important. If Holland couldn't get to the garden from the court—or anywhere else for that matter—or back again, without getting past here—"

"Right past this very spot," Holland interposed, smiling.

"And if Horder didn't see him either come or go—then he's wiped out of our reckoning."

He looked round the circle. There was general assent on the faces of the others.

"Well then, Holland—you might get on with your job."

"If I can be of any help—?"

"You heard nothing? No shot?"

Holland shook his head.

"Not likely I would, from the court," he said. "Thick walls— and I was hard at it. Anyhow, I heard nothing till Mr. Horder came."

With that he took his departure.

"See the door to the court is shut," Kershaw said to Sam; and Sam, descending quickly, saw that both doors to the dock were closed. As he came up again he stumbled and put down a hand to save himself. His hand touched the second step from the top, and as he recovered himself he picked up, almost without knowing it, a little twist of paper; equally vaguely he thrust it into his pierrot pocket. He took his place again in the group, nodding a silent answer to Kershaw's questioning look.

The latter took a deep breath, almost a sigh.

"Didn't want to talk in front of him. This is—well, you might call it a family affair."

Lawrence raised his eyebrows.

"Evidently," he said. "You, Mr. Kershaw, must take part in the conference. And Miss Brown and Mr. Horder. But—Mr. Burton? Has he joined my family?"

Burton flushed angrily and half smothered an ejaculation. There was a general restless movement.

"Steady," said Kershaw. "This is a pretty serious business. Let's go at it as calmly as we can."

"Calmly! When my brother—"

"I know." There was grave sympathy as well as firmness in Kershaw's voice. "Isn't that why? If we can get some idea before the police come—"

He looked steadily at Lawrence.

"You are right," he agreed slowly. "I will do my best. And— well, if it *is* a family affair," (and despite his promise he shot a menacing look at Burton) "the less we have to do with the police the better."

"It's a matter for the police all right," Kershaw said. "It's murder."

Again the thin eyebrows were raised; Lawrence's lips curled, very slightly, in a sneering smile.

"That may depend on me. We are in France, and I—" He shrugged his shoulders; it seemed, suddenly, to Samuel that he had dropped all the English veneer.

Kershaw stared at him, in a puzzled, almost a shocked, silence. Then, "You know best," he said. "Let's see where we stand. Now, Horder."

CHAPTER X

WHERE IS THE WEAPON?

"WELL," SAID SAM, "all I know is this. Ver—Miss Brown and I were sitting on this sofa," (and in spite of the tragedy which enveloped them all he reddened as he spoke) "and first of all Madame de Vigny came along with Burton. They went into the Tower."

An ejaculation from Lawrence: Kershaw quickly interposed a question.

"Were they talking?"

Doubtless the intention of the question was admirable, but Sam found it somewhat embarrassing. Lawrence again began to speak in a hot, angry tone, but Kershaw firmly begged him to be silent.

"Yes," Sam said at length, "they were talking. But what they said—"

Verity came suddenly to the rescue.

"I think I remember," she said, looking meaningly at the young man, "Mr. Burton was saying that he couldn't stand any more dancing."

"Oh yes, I remember now."

"And where did you go?" Lawrence demanded of his wife. "Found a nice quiet sitting-out place, I suppose?"

"Let's hear Horder's story first," Kershaw insisted, and Samuel hurriedly continued.

"Then your brother came along. At least, we weren't sure it was your brother. You see, his fancy dress and mask—"

"Who else could it have been? Or who did you think it might be?"

"Well—you. Anyhow," (he went on even more hurriedly), "whoever it was went into the Tower too, and we heard the noise of the door being opened into the garden, you know. Then Miss Brown went up to the gallery there because we weren't sure—I mean we wondered—"

He floundered hopelessly. The sneer on Lawrence's face became more pronounced.

"I think I see," he said. "You thought I might be looking for my wife."

"Certainly not," Sam answered, with more indignation than conviction. He dared not look at Margaret de Vigny or her sister, though he was conscious that they were listening with strained, almost horror-stricken attention. "Miss Brown had just got to the top of the steps," he continued, "when Miss Daubeney arrived. They exchanged a few words—"

He stopped short, with a start; a queer croaking sound came from Joan. Again Verity came to the rescue.

"Joan asked where Louis was. So then I knew who it was in the pierrot dress, and told her he was waiting for her in the garden. So she ran on after him. Then *you* came, Mr. Kershaw, and we—heard that scream. Joan's scream."

"Now it's my show.' Kershaw promptly took up the thread. "I ran down. No, that's wrong. First Burton and Madame de Vigny came out from the Tower and said there was something up in the garden."

"I insist on knowing." Lawrence's voice was really determined. "Did they come down the stairs or up?"

"Your wife and I came down from the room at the top of the Tower," Burton told him, defiantly.

"Oh, I see—" Lawrence began.

"I didn't—and don't," Kershaw broke in again. "I went down to the garden. Bang opposite me was Miss Daubeney, kneeling down by a body. Burton came with me. I took off the mask—unlooped it at one side, you know. It didn't take a second to see that your brother was dead. I told Burton to take Miss Daubeney away. I made a quick look round."

He paused dramatically, though with no such intent.

"I'm not a doctor or anything. But I'd stake my bottom dollar he was killed by a rifle bullet. Small bore. The temple. He had fallen where he was shot—hadn't been dragged or anything, I mean. Right in the angle of the wall. That seemed to me to mean he'd been shot from the garden side—in fact he couldn't have been shot from anywhere else. There *are* loopholes, but much too high. Above his head. And he wouldn't have fallen like that. You see how important the angle of the wall became. I took a sight along it, as well as I could. It gave me a V-shaped space of the garden; no window was possible—except the Tower. Yes, Pantaloon's Tower. That limits the field at once. Either someone in the garden, or someone in the Tower, or someone on the roof, perhaps, of the tennis-court or of this building."

"There's no way to either roof, unless by climbing," said Lawrence. "And there's no window from the tennis-court on to the garden, apart from the five little openings right up by the roof—quite inaccessible. So you see? There is not only the remote possibility of someone having climbed in—and out—over the outer wall."

"We need daylight to examine the ground at the foot of the wall outside," said Kershaw. "But the chances are that no one climbed out of the garden. There's that old man by the railings. He told us, didn't he, that he saw your brother come out?—the opening of the door, and the light streaming out caught his eye. And he heard a shot, he thinks. He couldn't see what happened—that's where the wall-angle comes in again. But he saw Miss Daubeney come out and he heard her scream and he saw the rest of us. What he didn't see was anyone climb over the wall—and he thinks he certainly would have done."

He paused.

"Well?" Burton demanded fiercely, voicing a general inquiry.

"Don't you see? Where's the weapon? You, Billie, were in the Tower, with Madame de Vigny. Miss Daubeney was in the garden, or at the foot of the Tower."

"D'you mean to suggest—?"

"Steady, old man."

"Why not?" Lawrence demanded. "Did you think it was Louis—or me?"

"You—"

"Quiet!" Kershaw shouted furiously. "Try to remember—"

Margaret and Joan had risen to their feet; it was perhaps the presence of the two women as much as Kershaw's domination which restrained the two men's fury.

"I accuse no one. But—before we go back to the Château let's be sure none of you three has got a weapon."

Margaret smiled wanly yet scornfully.

"Where am I to conceal a rifle—or Joan—in these dresses?" she asked.

"Why not a pistol?" Lawrence said. "We're not sure—"

"Verity can search us," Margaret suggested.

To Sam's secret indignation Kershaw agreed.

"We must protect ourselves," he said, rather apologetically.

Margaret led the way to the first of the two dressing-rooms and unlocked the door. As it shut behind them, "Horder," Kershaw ordered, "you can search Burton."

Samuel summoned to his aid his recollection of "crook films" and did his best to imitate the perfect sleuth.

"No weapon," he reported.

After the briefest of intervals the three women reappeared and Verity gave a similar negative report. Kershaw drew a deep breath.

"That leaves only Miss Brown," he said.

"But she wasn't there." Sam spoke hotly.

"No," came the answer, wearily patient, "but we want to provide for everything, don't we? She's the only one of us who's been back to the Château since—it happened. Suppose she took over her pistol—"

"Rifle you said."

"And rifle I think—"

"She certainly didn't do that—"

"But if I'm wrong, well, she could have taken a pistol, I suppose."

"I'm sure I don't know how," Verity protested. "Anyhow, I went over the bridge as quick as I could, asked one of the men where Lawrence was, went straight upstairs and met him on the stairs. Didn't I, Lawrence?"

"You certainly met me on the stairs."

"H'm. Well, I expect that's good enough," Kershaw pronounced after a few seconds' thought. "And that's that, then. Puzzle, find the weapon."

Joan Daubeney suddenly began to laugh, clearly on the verge of hysterics.

"Mr. Kershaw," Margaret demanded quite fiercely, "can't we go now? This is so awful—"

"Yes, surely," Burton said, and Sam murmured his support. Lawrence stood silent, a cold smile on his face.

"Very well," said Kershaw. "Mind you, there'll be plenty of questions in the morning."

Sombrely they all climbed the stairs and crossed the bridge; Verity and Margaret half carried Joan; then came Kershaw and Burton; Sam, bringing up the rear with Lawrence, could just hear the two men in front of him conversing in whispers.

In the inner hall, two men-servants and two or three maids were waiting, with white, scared faces. The latter hurried forward to meet their mistress, and conducted her and the other two up the stairs. Halfway up, Margaret turned and smiled—at Burton, not at Lawrence; but her husband's attention was occupied at the moment by a remark which Kershaw was addressing to him, and he did not notice the little incident.

"Can you put Burton up?" was Kershaw's question. "A sofa somewhere!"

"What, under this roof? And my brother—"

Burton clearly had himself well in hand; no doubt the whispered talk with his friend was responsible.

"Not at my request," he said coldly. "But Kershaw thinks—"

"You must remember, the police are bound to ask—and if Burton did kill your brother—not that I imagine he did—don't you want to keep an eye on him?"

"Have a murderer roaming about all night?"

"Don't be afraid of that," Kershaw assured him with a smile. Samuel felt that the whole business was outrageous; he could not decide which of the three men showed the most abominable lack of taste.

"My idea," went on the little man, "is that you, Monsieur de Vigny, Horder and I—the three people who are outside all suspicion—should do a bit of search work. All night, if need be."

A short silence.

"Very well," said Lawrence, and summoning one of the footmen he told him to conduct Mr. Burton to the library.

"It's quite comfortable," he said. "Even a fire. And some drinks. And a sofa. But the windows are barred. And—you can have whatever you like for breakfast. That's the tradition, I believe."

His tone robbed even his first words of any pretence at courtesy or friendliness, and he almost smacked his lips over his conclusion. Burton, however, thanked him gravely, nodded to Sam, and shook hands with Kershaw.

"Good night, Dandy old man. Good hunting."

"Good night, Billie. Sorry not to have you with me."

Burton walked steadily in the wake of the footman, without a backward glance.

"And now, Monsieur de Vigny," Kershaw turned to him, "before we start work, will you post that other footman here. In this hall. He's to tell you—or me—if anyone comes downstairs, or into this hall."

"What is the idea? D'you suppose they'll run away to-night?"

A contemptuous glance was the answer which Lawrence received.

"But I don't see—" Sam began.

"There's still the possibility," Kershaw explained patiently, "that Miss Brown did hide a pistol. I don't think so, but we must guard against it. If she did, then she—or one of them—will come and get it, or try to."

"I see," Sam confessed humbly, and Lawrence too nodded and began from that moment to recover something of his former friendly and helpful attitude towards the little man who was showing such an ability to grasp the essentials of a complicated situation.

Whilst the instructions were being transmitted to the footman, Kershaw took a cigarette from a big silver box and lit it. Sam followed his example, and also made an effort to wipe his forehead, becoming conscious that it was streaming with sweat. He had to unbutton his pierrot dress, and it occurred to him that it was no more than decent to discard it altogether. As he began to extricate himself he looked questioningly at his "commanding officer."

"Of course," said Kershaw with a smile.

As Sam pushed the dress down over his hips he stopped with a sudden exclamation and thrust his hand into his trousers pocket.

"What is it?" asked Kershaw sharply, and Lawrence, dismissing the footman to his new duty, also turned quickly round.

Sam produced, with a sheepish smile, the key of the padlock which fastened the boat in the little dock. He explained hastily what it was and how he came to have it about him.

"But is it of any importance?" asked Lawrence.

"I hadn't thought of a boat," Kershaw admitted.

"No—no, I suppose it doesn't help."

"Certainly not," Lawrence stated positively. "You can't possibly land inside the Château except at the dock, and you can't get from the dock to the kitchen garden without going through the gallery where you and Verity were. No one *did* go through in either direction, except the people you've told us?"

"No one."

His answer was so firm and confident that it carried conviction.

"Your friend, Kershaw—he's the man," Lawrence said, with hardly less conviction. "I shall shoot him to-morrow morning."

Good Lord, said Sam to himself, he's got a duel in his mind: I thought he was merely contemplating the hangman.

"Shoot Broadside Burton; more likely he—" The little man stopped short, and swore under his breath.

"Thank you," said Lawrence, his sneer coming back to his lips. "That's what I thought. A crack shot, is he?"

The two men stared at one another in silence; the little man slowly shook his head.

"I'm not afraid to face possibilities," he answered. "But it's no more than a possibility. First of all—it wasn't you he shot; and secondly—where's the weapon?"

After a pause he went on briskly: "That's the first thing. We must hunt for a weapon. Likely to be a long job, so I suggest we begin with a drink. Takes it out of you, this sort of thing."

Without a word, Lawrence led the way towards the dining-room; the buffet, piled with food and bottles but silent and deserted, was another of the night's incongruities.

Samuel delayed a second or two. The footman standing at the foot of the stairs was paying no attention to him; he picked up the pierrot dress which he had discarded.

At the door of the dining-room Kershaw looked round. All that he saw was the young artist carefully folding up his black and white carnival dress; but in the pocket of the artist's evening trousers reposed that scrap of paper which he had picked up on the stairs. He had been reminded of it by the discovery of the key: it might be nothing, but on the other hand—

Carefully as he had folded up the dress, he laid it on a chair with a look of repugnance and hastened to join the other two. Silently he followed their example and poured himself a stiff whisky and soda.

"Kershaw," he said suddenly. "He's still lying out there. Black and white pierrot. Can't—can't we cover him up?"

The other bestowed on him a tolerant, sympathetic smile; perhaps even on so short an acquaintance it was possible to detect the "artistic temperament."

"Of course," he said.

Lawrence impulsively snatched from a sofa-back a heavy sheet of purple silk.

"Come on," he said.

CHAPTER XI

RIDDLES AND KEYS

IT SEEMED to Sam that the nightmare in which he was living took a turn, and, in spite of the horror through which he had passed, for the worse. No doubt the reaction left him limp; he suddenly became conscious that physically he was exhausted. And Kershaw evidently was bent on a thorough and prolonged examination.

As they recrossed the bridge, Kershaw observed that there was no longer a light in the tennis-court—at any rate, none shone from the crack below the door.

"I might put back the boat-key," Sam suggested. "That is, if the door of the court isn't locked."

Lawrence, recalled from a sombre abstraction, said that it was never locked; so Sam went down and with the aid of a match or two, since he could not find the switch, replaced the key at long last on its hook.

The other two waited for him on the upper gallery.

"What—what do we do now?" he asked, as he rejoined them.

"The Tower," was Kershaw's curt reply,

"No. First—this," Lawrence firmly contradicted him, and indicated the silk hanging on his arm. The other acquiesced, with a gentle wave of his hand, palm upturned, which somehow was a respectful version of a shrug of the shoulders. Their progress down the twisting turret stairs, where the electric light still burnt, took on the character of a procession. At the foot the man "on guard" stood respectfully aside.

Kershaw touched Lawrence's arm; the latter checked and turned, an angry, hurt look in his eyes.

"Just ask him if he's seen anything, or anyone, will you?"

"*Rien du tout,* monsieur," the man answered, with a shake of his head.

Kershaw nodded. They walked on towards the figure lying so still in the angle of the wall. Kershaw and Samuel stopped short—a yard or two away. For a moment one black and white pierrot

stood stiffly upright, staring down at his black and white counterpart at his feet. Then with a gesture which had something of the
Middle Ages in it, he swept the purple pall over the body. He
whispered something, so softly that the other two could not hear
what he said. Then he turned, took a pace or two forward towards
his two companions, his face white but resolute.

"And now—to business."

His tone was deliberately as matter of fact as his words.

"You see," said Kershaw, "if he fell where he was shot—and
he was not dragged here, and he couldn't have walked—then the
angle of the wall fixes the area from within which the shot was
fired."

"And if he was carried?" Lawrence asked.

"Yes. There's that to be thought of. But we needn't discuss that
out here. I don't think it's likely myself, but—well, it depends on
what the others saw, doesn't it?"

Lawrence's upward sweep of his hands was wholly a Gallic
expression of exasperation.

"I must remember Burton is your friend," he said.

"Yes, but Madame de Vigny was there. She'd have seen it."
Samuel thought it was time he took part in the conversation.

"That, too," was the answer, "we will discuss—at the right time
and place. How far the testimony of my wife—"

"And Joan—Miss Daubeney, I mean," Sam went on, rather
hastily. He had, perhaps, no right to resent what Lawrence might
choose to think or say about his wife, but the most correct young
man cannot always do the right thing.

"That's so," Kershaw supported him. "We haven't asked
them—any of them—just what they saw or how they saw it."

"Or where exactly they were," Lawrence agreed.

"Still, there's the old man by the railings. He did not and could
not see your brother fall—so even if he was moved, it wasn't far.
He must have been in the angle—if not at its apex. And secondly,
he heard the shot and *afterwards* saw Miss Daubeney come out
from the Tower—that's so, isn't it?" he appealed to Lawrence,
who nodded.

"I don't see why Burton—or either of the others—should have
wanted to move the body to a place which made it more certain
than otherwise it would have been that the shot came from a certain direction."

"No," said Sam. "More likely someone else would do that—I
mean to say, if he had been shot in the middle of the garden."

"Which, if old Pierre is telling the truth, he wasn't. And there's no reason why Pierre should lie, is there?"

"I've no idea," said Kershaw. "That's a point for the police, I should say. If the old man had a grudge against your brother—or you—"

"Me?"

"Well, it's possible someone mistook your brother for you. Or even that they thought that to kill your brother was a good enough way to pay on a score of yours."

Lawrence jerked his head and looked haughtily at the little man.

"Bosh," he said. "I've known old Pierre since I was a boy. So had—Louis. A friend of ours."

Still, thought Samuel to himself, Kershaw is right. The police must look into this.

Kershaw abandoned this topic and returned to stare at Pantaloon's Tower. The light streamed out from the doorway and from the three windows nearly straight above it; for in the turret room as well as the staircase, the lights apparently had been left burning.

"Miss Daubeney may have seen it from a window or from the door or even from the garden," he said, though she was hardly likely, he reflected, to have looked out of the second window, the one so much below eye-level.

"Seen what?"

"Seen your brother fall."

"If she did actually see it," Sam interposed.

"You mean, he may have fallen before she got into the garden but not whilst she was at a window?"

"Yes."

"That's so. We'll ask her to-morrow. I'm not sure it matters. What *does* matter is, I think, that we can check Burton's movements by hers. I mean he *must* have been a stage behind her, so to speak. And Madame de Vigny too."

"I see," Sam agreed. "If Miss Daubeney saw it from the window, Burton must have been in the turret room."

"What's the point of all this?" Lawrence demanded impatiently. "We haven't asked them yet. And for that matter, Burton may have been in the doorway; Joan may have seen him shoot Louis—"

"Good God, sir, how can you—" the artist broke out.

"Really!" the other's very tone silenced him. "Must I remind you that my brother has been murdered? That is so incredible that—nothing else is more difficult to believe, my friend."

His voice broke a little as he concluded, and Samuel felt quite apologetic. All the same to suggest that Joan Daubeney—Verity's friend—

"Well," said Kershaw, relieving the tension, "I expect we're wasting time. What we want is—the weapon. We can't search the garden properly till the morning; all we can do is to ensure that no one gets in and takes it away."

"The two watchmen will do that," Lawrence observed, and Kershaw agreed.

"So that leaves the Tower itself."

They entered it. It was not difficult to establish the fact that no weapon had been left on the actual stairs; they were bare and narrow, and on the whole very well lit by the electric lights; and where the shadows were fairly heavy, it was enough to strike a match. So they came to the turret room.

It was a little round room of no particular interest or distinction. Its furniture consisted of an old, rather ragged carpet, a round table, three stiff-looking chairs, and two or three indifferent prints on the bare walls. There was no cupboard of any kind. Kershaw stood and surveyed it, preventing them from entering.

"H'm, no weapon here," he said; and then with, it seemed, a special significance for Lawrence de Vigny's benefit, he went on:

"Madame de Vigny apparently sat one side of the table—there, facing the window. And Burton sat opposite, with his back to it. You see? He sat in that chair because there's the ash of his cigar on the carpet; and Madame de Vigny sat in one or other of the two chairs this side."

Lawrence gave an impatient snort, and tried to push Kershaw on into the room.

"Go slow," the latter protested. "It will help us to check the stories they tell us."

"Perhaps they shared one chair," Lawrence suggested, offensively; the others ignored the remark. Kershaw advanced into the room and sat down first in one, then the other of the chairs either of which, he had said, Margaret de Vigny might have occupied.

"Can't see the angle of the wall from here," he observed. Then, "Hullo," he said, leaning forward and looking at something which was lying on the table. The other two came forward to inspect the discovery. With much care he picked up a half-smoked cigar; then he scrutinized the table.

"See that?" he asked. Burton put down his cigar, still burning, and left it there when he left the room."

"Yes," said Samuel, rather blankly.

"Don't you think," the little man answered the question which obviously was implied by the blank tone and expression, "that it suggests that he put it down quietly and calmly enough—and then got hustled and forgot it?"

"Put it down carefully while he took aim," Lawrence commented, "and forgot it in the excitement of—hitting the target."

This time it was Kershaw who snorted.

"One thing's obvious," he said. "If the shot was fired from here, it wasn't fired from a revolver. Too far in this light."

"But don't you say yourself it was a rifle?"

"Yes. And that brings us right up against it. Where's the rifle?"

It certainly was very easy for them to satisfy themselves that no rifle could possibly be concealed in the turret room. It seemed equally certain that no one had gone out on to the roof of the tennis-court through the door in the turret room—the only way of access to it, as Lawrence said. For the door was bolted, and the bolts were thick in cobwebs. Nevertheless, they went out on to the roof to make sure.

"I can't see what's left—except the garden," was Kershaw's final conclusion. And even Lawrence, despite his obvious prejudice, was unable to put forward any other theory.

"So there we are," Kershaw finally pronounced. "And we can't do any more good here to-night. We'd best move back to the house."

They followed him in silence, down the stairs and on to the upper gallery. There Lawrence stopped them.

"My brother," he said. "Lying out there."

Kershaw shook his head.

"Better not," he replied, sympathetically yet firmly. "The police will surely want to see everything exactly as it was."

"The police!" Lawrence said with angry scorn. "God knows when they'll condescend to leave the Carnival and attend to—this."

They went on across the bridge; Samuel dragged wearily in the rear, and was thankful to observe that their course took them back to the buffet. On the way Lawrence asked the footman on duty in the hall if anyone had been there: "*Non,* monsieur!"

Still in almost unbroken silence they consumed three stiff whiskies and soda. Samuel glanced surreptitiously at his watch and saw with amazement that it was going on for three o'clock. The whisky gave him courage to suggest that it was high time he and Kershaw made their way back to the hotel.

"Burton's staying here, I gather," he concluded.

Kershaw glanced at him queerly.

"I think I'll stay here, too, if M. de Vigny will let me. Until the police come. Besides—it won't look so much as if Burton were under arrest, so to speak."

He turned and looked Lawrence straight in the face, in a kind of silent duel. The latter lowered his eyes first and rather grudgingly assented.

"Oh, well, then, perhaps I'd better stay too. I can sleep in an arm-chair," Samuel gallantly volunteered.

"Sleep!" said Lawrence. "My God, sleep! I wish *I* could."

"We'll none of us sleep too well," Kershaw put in. "But I don't see why Horder should sit up. It's different for him."

And so it was finally settled.

"You can get out through the tennis-court," Lawrence suggested, apologetically. "Kershaw will let you out. I'm sure you'll forgive me. I'll get the key."

"Of course," Sam said.

They went back to the inner hall. Lawrence walked over towards a grandfather clock and took down a key from a hook beside it. He stopped, the hand that held the key suspended in mid-air.

"That's funny," he said. "The other key's gone."

"What other key?"

"One that's very seldom used. Opens the gate in those iron railings."

"Good Lord!" Kershaw cried, in sudden excitement. "That alters the whole position. When was it taken?"

"How should I know?"

"Miss Brown may be able to help," Sam suggested, a shade diffidently. "She used the tennis-court key to let me out. But that was yesterday. Of course, how stupid of me! Any number of people may have used it since then."

"Why not ask the footman?" was Kershaw's suggestion. Lawrence shrugged his shoulders.

"Very well," he said. "It's not likely he'll know. He isn't always on duty at the foot of the stairs."

He asked the man whether he was sure that no one had entered the hall, and explained that the key was missing. The man's expression passed from indignation through surprise to thoughtfulness. Suddenly he burst out excitedly. Kershaw could not make head or tail of what he said; Sam was too weary to gather more than a word here and there. They waited for Lawrence to interpret.

"He suggests that Louis took it," he informed them. "Sounds absurd to me, but he swears that he was here, or rather came through here, carrying a tray, just when Louis came downstairs in fancy dress; and he remembers he saw him walk over to the clock and reach up towards those pegs. He can't swear he took down a key but—Still, I can't believe it. Why should Louis want the key?"

"To go out," Samuel brightly suggested: then he blushed, not so much because of the platitudinous nature of the suggestion as because like a flash of lightning an idea sprang into his mind.

The other two men stared at him, Lawrence with that scornful air of his, Kershaw with the ghost of a smile of amusement.

And then Samuel had yet another inspiration.

"Sorry to be so obvious. What I meant was, suppose he wanted to buy something from the old man by the railings? You know, he—or someone else when he was there—said something to me about balloons and false noses. At least I'm pretty sure he was there."

"I see," Kershaw spoke thoughtfully. "It's an idea, anyhow."

"Not a very good one," Lawrence argued. "There's nothing old Pierre sells that couldn't be handed through the bars. Except balloons, it's true. Well, it's possible, I admit. Anyhow, if Louis took the key, the matter is of less importance."

"Yes, *if* he did," Kershaw agreed. "That's to say, if he took it and put it in his pocket and it's still there. Then the question why he took it may matter or it may not. But if it isn't there—then I shall begin to wonder whether your old friend Pierre is telling the truth. You see, it gives a way of escape from the garden."

There was a silence.

"Ought—ought we to make sure?" Sam asked.

"*No!*" The monosyllable came explosively from Lawrence's lips. "If the body has to lie out there all night—at least let it lie undisturbed."

Kershaw lifted one eyebrow, in a way which provoked a further argument.

"Without the police, and in the middle of the Carnival—well, even if the key has gone, it's no use our chasing on to try and catch the man who took it."

This indeed could not be gainsaid. Few more words were exchanged before Lawrence handed over the tennis-court key and held out his hand to Samuel.

"Good night, Horder," he said. "Thank you. I'm sorry you are mixed up in this horrible business."

Sam could find no words in which to answer. He wrung his host's hand, picked up his fancy dress and turned to follow Kershaw across the bridge once more.

"I'll wait for you here," Lawrence called after the latter.

This time they found the switch immediately inside the tennis-court, but beyond that they plunged on in darkness. A match showed them the "postern gate." Kershaw opened it, and as Samuel slipped out laid his hand for a moment on his shoulder. He bade him good night in a warm, friendly tone, which seemed to thank him for having stood by the speaker and—

"I'll be up in the morning," Sam said, and stumbled down the steps. The door shut behind him with a sharp snap.

As Samuel groped his way along the path, past the cottage—dark and silent—and down to the road, one thought kept running in his mind—the recollection of the words he had heard amongst those very trees on his first night at St. André; and then the bathing party when Louis had been so tactless, and Joan Daubeney so angry—

He staggered rather than walked into the hotel. He was surprised that the door was still open and a light burning in the lounge. It was not till the night-porter spoke to him—in English, if hardly recognizable as such—and expressed the hope that Monsieur had amused himself well, that he remembered the Carnival.

The night-porter watched the young Englishman's progress up the stairs with an understanding smile.

"Doubtless," he thought, "the wine at the Château is of the first order."

CHAPTER XII

THE MORNING AFTER

"THUD, THUD, THUD . . . Samuel became aware that he had just woken up from an unpleasant nightmare, though he had been too deeply asleep to remember what it was all about, that it was broad daylight and that someone was knocking at his door. Oh, yes, he was in the Hotel Splendide at St. André-sur-Mer, and last night . . . He bade the knocker come in.

It was the *concierge,* beaming with smiles.

"These have been brought by hand from the Château, monsieur," and he laid something down on the table beside the bed, and withdrew. Samuel blinked and groaned; heaved himself up in bed and looked at his watch with one half-open eye. Apparently, however, he had forgotten to wind it up overnight. What was all this about the Château? Oh, yes; a note.

He tore it clumsily open and read it through twice before he grasped what it was all about. It was simple enough: a note from Kershaw asking him to send up to the Château, by the bearer, a few clothes and a razor or so, for himself and Burton. A postscript added "De Vigny says will you come up in the course of the morning?"

Samuel dragged himself out of bed, donned slippers and the dressing-gown which suggested that his name ought rather to have been Joseph, and rang the bell. Whilst waiting for it to be answered he hastily splashed some cold water over his head and brushed his hair.

He had of course rung the bell the wrong number of times. He explained to the chambermaid who answered it what it was he wanted. She departed for reinforcements and he sat down, yawning, on the edge of the bed. And then he saw that the *concierge* had brought two notes—he remembered that the man had used the plural tense. He picked up the second and stared at it in puzzlement, then opened it and looked at the signature. Verity! The name accelerated the "waking-up" process. She gathered, the note said, that Mr. Kershaw, on Lawrence's behalf, had asked Sam to come up during the morning. Would he be there by ten o'clock? And if he would come by the tennis-court, she would be on the look-out for him.

Ten o'clock! Good Lord, what was the time now? Fortunately the chambermaid reappeared at the moment, accompanied by the *concierge,* and together they reported that it was only about a quarter to nine. The *concierge* hinted that, the day after the Carnival, that was a very early hour.

Sam explained Kershaw's request, and the *concierge* smiled and remarked knowingly, "so the two gentlemen stayed the night at the Château. » The news of the tragedy evidently had not yet reached St. André-sur-Mer.

Sam was conducted first to Kershaw's and then to Burton's room, and in each selected what seemed to him a sufficient outfit for the circumstances (it is true that he selected for Kershaw only half a pair of sock-suspenders and for Burton no tie, but these were genuine accidents). He stuffed the things into one good-sized suitcase of Burton's and directed that it should be handed over to the footman for conveyance to the Château, together with a verbal message that he himself would follow in due course. Then he ordered a *café complet* to be brought to his room in twenty minutes' time.

He lingered a few minutes in Burton's room, for he wanted to examine an object which had caught his eye, in a drawer. It was a small but serviceable automatic pistol. Was it likely that a more or less casual traveller would go about with two weapons? This one certainly could not have been in its owner's keeping at the dance the previous night. Of course, Burton had gone in to the town—or had not Kershaw gone with him? Anyway, they might both be "in" it, and if so it would explain Kershaw's keen interest. But then would anyone be fool enough to buy a rifle or a pistol locally— and the "anyone" in this case was a foreigner, too?

But what was the use of such meditations? Speed was called for—a shave and a hasty bathe were what he needed. He hurried back to his own room.

Everything, of course, went wrong. The water in the hot tap was less than lukewarm—curse the Carnival! The maid took longer than usual to answer the bell; by the time the hot water came he had finished lathering—with cold water; and finally he contrived to inflict on himself one of those unpleasant torn cuts of which only a safety-razor seems capable.

This left him about five minutes for his bathe—assuming, of course, that his coffee and rolls were going to appear punctually. No one was stirring outdoors, though he caught a glimpse of the old couple who had been at the hotel when first he arrived, waiting gloomily for their breakfast in the *salle à manger.* He fairly hurled himself into the sea, and thereby severely stubbed a big toe. The cold sea water however was most invigorating. He wrapped his bath-gown round him and hustled, dripping, back to the hotel and to his room. And then, of course, the coffee was late, so he decided he would get dressed before it came; and then it came when he was half dressed, so he decided to finish before he tackled it, and when he did he found that it was nearly cold.

When he had gulped it down and consumed the rolls—actually they were none too fresh, but the honey helped—he made some effort to tidy up his room. His evening clothes were lying all over the place, as he had flung them on when he had come in. As he folded the trousers he felt something in one of the pockets; he extracted that little twisted piece of paper which he had picked up on the steps and which he had entirely forgotten to examine.

He unfolded it now. It was a very ordinary scrap of cheap paper, with a few words pencilled on it. "L. Look at 2350."

He puzzled over it for a while, but could make nothing of it. He had hoped—or feared—to find something which identified it with Joan Daubeney, on a wild theory that her clenched hand as she hurried after Louis, had contained some note or other. But—well, if the message had anything at all to do with the affair, it seemed to have been addressed to Louis, not to Joan. As for the message itself, he could not imagine what it meant.

He put it away in his pocket-book, though he had half a mind to chuck it away. He looked at his watch. If he had been given the right time when he set it, then he must hurry up, for it was nearly a quarter to ten.

He ran down into the hall and set out at a round pace for the Château. Mrs. Holland was in the garden of the cottage and bade him good morning with a kind of subdued vivacity—a mixed tribute to the living and the dead.

"Isn't it *terrible* about poor dear Mr. Louis?" she said. "Such an awful thing. Len told me about it last night—no Carnival for us, you know; we're quiet folk—and I could hardly sleep for thinking of it."

Sam found some difficulty in replying—considering what he knew, the woman was loathsomely callous. Perhaps his manner betrayed something of his feelings; at all events, Mrs. Holland's conversation ended rather abruptly and stiffly.

"You'll find my husband up at the court," she said. "Though I don't suppose there'll be much tennis for some time."

He struggled on up the sandy path, found the door open and entered the dedans and was overjoyed to find Verity—a pale weary-looking Verity—waiting for him. Mindful (as he hoped she was too) of the state of their relations before last night's tragedy he advanced with both hands outstretched.

But, "Good morning, Sam," she said, in a cool level tone and as she did so glanced over her shoulder into the court. Holland was there, busy with a large broom. So the artist was left uncertain whether her coolness was to be accounted for by the presence of a third person or whether her ardour of last night had been due to the Carnival spirit.

"Come over into the garden," she went on, "so that we can talk. Before the others know you're here."

"Kershaw's expecting me, you know."

"He's with the police still. Come on."

Little more was said. From the Tower at the far side of the bridge it was possible to escape directly into the garden without going through the hall, and Verity chose this route, leading the way to a secluded corner of the battlements, overlooking the Old Town. Yet even there Samuel failed to secure convincing evidence that Holland's presence in the court had been the restraining influence.

"Sam, isn't this too *ghastly?*" she said, and for a while their conversation consisted of jerky references to the events of the night before.

"Louis was such a dear," she said.

"Seemed a very good fellow. Awful for all of you. And—er—especially for Joan."

She looked at him with a hint of surprise in her expression.

"Why Joan? You don't mean—oh, but I don't think she felt like that about him. I don't say that—well, a bit of flirtation, isn't that the expression? But it wasn't more than that. Yes, I'm sure. Not as far as she was concerned anyhow. I don't know about him. Perhaps he—And I think Margaret rather hoped—"

Samuel was frankly astonished, and a little annoyed. This further upset the theory to which he was beginning to attach himself; nothing is more irritating to your amateur investigator than to have his pet and airiest theory upset by another person's presentation of the facts. He said as much—very discreetly, and was promptly requested to explain exactly what he meant.

This he did not altogether do, for he said nothing about his piece of paper, nor yet the voices in the wood: naturally, perhaps, since the paper failed to support his theory. Consequently he had by now pretty well made up his mind that it had nothing to do with the case. Still, he did, hesitatingly, argue that when Joan spoke to Verity on the upper gallery her tone suggested that she was anything but amiable.

"Don't you remember?" he urged his companion. "Didn't she say in so many words that Louis had gone to meet someone else in the garden? And if she was in love with him—"

Miss Brown was heartless enough to laugh.

"My poor Samuel," she said mockingly, "what queer ideas you have of your countrywomen. Joan's English, you know—not a refugee from Corsica or something like that."

"But—but didn't you think she was jolly angry?"

"I dare say. And I dare say, too, that Lawrence—he's a Latin after all—would think as you do. But I know Joan. She's like me—and if you expect me to murder you because you sit out with someone else instead of me—well, you'd better think again, my dear."

"I see," said Sam, "I expect you're right."

In justice to him, it must be said that he felt vastly relieved, even though the relief came at the expense of his own little theory. Then he grew gloomy again.

"But if—if it wasn't Joan—"

"How *could* it have been?"

"The weapon, you mean? I know. But that's a kind of general difficulty."

"Well, neither Joan nor Margaret had a pistol or a rifle or a howitzer hidden on her. You can take my word for that."

Samuel looked at her thoughtfully.

"Sure?" he said, and added hastily, to avert her wrath: "You see we both of us—well, avoided the exact truth last night, didn't we?"

Verity laughed.

"I suppose we did, and we're sticking to the same story, aren't we? But honestly, Sam—you know I'd *tell you* the whole truth, don't you?"

And Sam was happily—and rightly—certain that this was so.

"Well then," he resumed, "if it wasn't Joan, that leaves either Madame de Vigny or Burton, doesn't it? You see, Burton might have thought it was Lawrence, not Louis—"

"But *Sam,*" Verity cried, in genuine consternation, "you must be mad. To think that Margaret would have stood by and let Mr. Burton—Oh, I see," and again she laughed. "My lad, you're on the wrong track again. It's quite true Lawrence is liable to be jealous of Margaret—he's got a strong possessive sense, you know—but Margaret is just as liable to be jealous of him. Why, she's devoted to him. Much more than he is to her, I should say."

Samuel positively goggled at her.

"But—but—I thought—" he stammered. "I heard Burton say—you know, he wanted to marry her ages ago."

Verity in turn looked startled, but she quickly collected herself.

"That doesn't say she wanted to marry *him,*" she observed, and Samuel's recollection of the talk which he had overheard in Paris was not certain enough to enable him to continue the argument. So he changed the conversation by asking how Margaret and Joan were.

"Well, of course, they're both terribly upset," she said, "so are all of us. And Lawrence. He feels it most of all. Of course it was his only brother but—honestly I'd no idea he was so fond of him. They got on very well on the whole of course, but—"

She shrugged her shoulders: Sam in his own mind agreed that so far as his small acquaintance with the brothers went, they had seemed rather inclined to squabble.

"Possessive sense again, I dare say," he hazarded. "I should think he's dead keen to get the murderer caught."

"I suppose so," Verity agreed, but a trifle dubiously, and Sam looked at her questioningly. "Oh, I wasn't thinking so much of Lawrence. I've hardly seen him to talk to. What I meant was, it doesn't seem much good to catch the murderer and hang him, does it? It wouldn't bring Louis back to life."

The artist remembered that he had read a good deal in the English papers some time before on the subject of the value of capital punishment and his general recollection was that its advocates usually got the worst of the argument. He had no wish to be driven to what he considered a purely feminine method of opposing "I'm *sure I'm* right," to proofs that logically he was wrong; so he let the subject drop. Instead, he said that he supposed he ought to go and see Kershaw.

They found Kershaw was sitting in a chair in the inner hall. He jumped up as they entered.

"Ah, there you are, Horder. You've been the devil of a time coming here." He spoke impatiently; then his eye twinkled and he apologized to Verity—ostensibly for the language.

"What's the hurry?" Sam inquired innocently.

"The police are here. They came up eventually last night, of course, or rather in the small hours. But they only started in on their examination of the witnesses and so on a couple of hours ago. I've told them all I know, and they want to see you."

"Yes, but I don't know any more—"

"You can corroborate what I've told 'em. And as a matter of fact a lot of what I told 'em is only what you told me. About who went into Pantaloon's Tower and so on."

Without more ado, he bustled Samuel along to the library. He opened the door without ceremony, announced, "Here's Horder," and thrust him in. Sam found himself looking at Lawrence de Vigny, rising from a large arm-chair to greet him.

He looked completely worn out, but managed a faint smile, and proceeded to introduce him to two of the other occupants of the room. One was obviously a gendarme—Sam judged he was something like a sergeant—and the other presumably was the Examining Magistrate; he was too confused by his sudden entry to take in the details of Lawrence's introduction. The magistrate, or Commissaire or whatever he was, bowed solemnly; he was most correctly garbed in a rather badly-fitting frock-coat. He reseated himself at the writing-table in front of the fireplace, whence he had risen to give his bow, and motioned Sam to occupy a chair facing him. The sergeant seated himself rather stiffly a little behind the gentleman in the frock-coat; another man, also in black clothes and palpably a clerk, was seated at a small table by the centre window. Lawrence dragged his own chair round, so that it was sideways to the big table.

"I'll interpret—where necessary," he said, and sat down in his turn.

The proceedings began with a quantity of formal questions. In accordance with tradition, Sam was facing the light; and the magistrate further added to the theatricality of the atmosphere by frowning severely and thrusting forward his head in a most uncomfortable attitude. Suddenly it dawned on the artist that the fellow imagined himself to be delivering "rapier glances" and all the rest of it. He was hard put to it to avoid smiling, especially when it further became apparent how much importance was attached to anything which Lawrence de Vigny said. He was treated with overwhelming deference, and Sam realized that the hints which Lawrence had thrown out overnight, about his own influence as a nobleman, even if he did not use his title, had their basis in solid fact.

However, it greatly simplified things, so far as Samuel was concerned. It seemed that he had been guilty of criminal negligence in failing to put his passport in his pocket—it might even have been thought that he ought never to be separated from it, even when bathing. "However, if Monsieur de Vigny vouches for it,"—and all was well. Then too his profession and the purpose of his visit to St. André—to be an artist was not, it seemed, a reasonable answer to both questions; but since he was a friend . . . At last they came to business, and here all was plain sailing. Samuel carefully repeated first of all the account which he had given to Kershaw and Lawrence of what he and Verity had seen in the gallery and then of the investigation which Kershaw had conducted.

Finally, the magistrate expressed himself as satisfied; he even went so far as to compliment Samuel.

"You haven't contradicted either yourself or anyone else," said Lawrence with a faint smile.

The magistrate smiled too, without a notion of what Lawrence had said; he felt that it was proper to do so.

CHAPTER XIII

THE DAWN OF THEORY

SAMUEL FOUND Verity and Kershaw in the inner hall; they had evidently been deep in conversation and were almost startled to see him. Kershaw rose to his feet, and as he did so he glanced meaningly at the girl. She too got up, slowly and reluctantly.

"All finished, Horder, as far as you're concerned?"

"Yes, apparently."

"Then Miss Brown is for it. Cheer up," he added, addressing her. "I promise you, they'll treat you like a duchess. She's all of a dither' (this to Samuel), "though I've done my best to get her to pull her socks up."

"It's perfectly all right, Verity," Sam assured her. "They'll just want you to say what we saw—same as last night."

She gave a deep sigh, half of resignation, half of alarm, and still hesitated.

"Do—do I just walk in? Won't they send out to say—"

"Walk right in," Kershaw laughed. "Don't I keep telling you this isn't a dentist's waiting-room? Come on."

He led the way: Samuel quietly caught Verity's hand as she passed him and squeezed it—perhaps to cheer her up, perhaps to remind her that she must "stick to the story.' Kershaw conducted her to the library and then came back, and the two men sat down in a couple of large arm-chairs—more comfortable than they looked—and lit up pipes.

They sat in silence for quite a little time, Kershaw smoking furiously and gazing into space. At last the artist could bear it no longer.

"Well?" he demanded, "what's happening? Where's Burton?"

Kershaw looked at him steadily or a couple of seconds before he answered.

"Burton's tucked away somewhere—no, not under arrest, but to some extent under suspicion. Nothing very serious, if you ask me; a sort of sop to de Vigny."

Sam looked at him questioningly.

"Oh, that will pass too," Kershaw answered the look. "I mean, de Vigny's attitude of mind. In fact, it's passing already, I reckon. Naturally he wants someone to go through it—and apparently he's jealous of Billie Burton, anyhow. All he had to do—and he did it—was to let fall a remark about Burton being a famous big-game hunter, 'Broadside Burton'—that's his nickname, you know."

"But don't you think that that fact means—?"

"That they'll charge him with murder? No, I don't. I guess they'll do a lot to please de Vigny—chiefly if he wanted things hushed up. But, you see, there's a snag they can't get round, when it comes to accusing Burton of the murder. And that is—what became of the weapon?"

"Nothing's been found in the garden?"

"Nothing. Not a sign of anyone having hidden it—or himself—in there. And what's more they've put that old fellow with the booth in the corner by the bridge through a kind of Third Degree—a pretty stiff one—and he's quite unshaken in his certainty that no one got into the kitchen garden from outside. And thirdly, they've examined the ground at the foot of the wall, on the outside. It's soft sand, and there's no mark of anyone climbing in or out. For that matter, I doubt whether it could be done without a ladder of some kind, and you wouldn't get a ladder there—or heave a rope and grapnel up—without leaving lots of traces."

Sam perhaps looked a little surprised at the dogmatic manner in which the other man made this assertion.

"You can take it from me that's so," Kershaw went on, however. "Don't forget that I'm a bit more used than you are—or these police either—to reading the meaning of marks on the ground."

The artist certainly had quite forgotten that he was talking to a man who was as much of a hunter as Burton himself. He wondered all of a sudden whether Kershaw . . .

A chuckle of unfeigned amusement interrupted his thoughts.

"No, I'm out of it," said Kershaw, and Sam reddened. "Miss Brown can swear that I was at the other end of the bridge—this end—when the shot was fired. Don't you remember—?"

"Of course," said Sam, and apologized. The other laughingly granted his forgiveness.

"You're quite right," he said, "to suspect anyone and every one."

Silence fell again—an oppressive silence which Sam felt must be ended at all costs. So much so that he was on the point of blurt-

ing out some of the things which he had kept back—the truth
about the conversation which he had overheard from the lower
gallery, or else that scrap of paper, relevant to the case or not—
when all of a sudden he bethought himself of another opening.

"I say, Kershaw, what about that key? You know, the one to the
door in the railings which the footman said poor Louis de Vigny
took with him."

"They found it in his pocket," was the brief reply.

"Oh." He ought, no doubt, to have expected the answer; nevertheless he was a good deal taken aback. "Then—then—no one
could have got in that way. I mean, Louis de Vigny wouldn't have
had time to go to the railings, let someone in and then—"

"Hurry back to the angle of the wall and get the new-comer to
shoot him, with a rifle, from the foot of the Tower. No, I don't
think that's possible. Besides, there's the evidence of the man at
the carnival stall—Pierre, you know."

"Of course. Yes. Then—why—?" And Samuel stammered his
way to a full stop. His companion looked at him curiously, almost
suspiciously.

"Why *what?*" he asked.

Sam in fact had suddenly seen the answer to the question he
had been on the brink of asking: why had Louis de Vigny taken
the key if not to admit someone? Obviously, to let someone else
out. And who was that someone but himself? And from that
sprang unnumbered possibilities—or impossibilities. It would
never do to set Kershaw thinking along those lines, or Joan
Daubeney . . .

Sam laughed, awkwardly.

"Why nothing," he said. "I wasn't going to ask a question exactly. I was just going to say the whole thing's absurd. No one *can*
have been in a position to fire that shot except Burton, Madame de
Vigny and Miss Daubeney. And quite apart from the absurdity of
thinking anyone of them *could* have done it, well, where's the
weapon, as you say?"

"That's it in a nutshell," Kershaw agreed.

"Of course, there's Holland," Sam suggested, almost hopefully.
"Oh, I know he couldn't have got into the garden from the tennis-
court without our seeing him—"

"Utterly impossible; he'd have had to come up the stairs within
a yard of you and then along the upper gallery. We even considered those tiny little windows right up at the top of the tennis-
court; but it's certain they couldn't be reached—not without a very

tall ladder. And there's no such thing in the place. No, that idea is impossible."

"I know," Sam admitted, despondent again. "It's just that it's odd his being there."

Kershaw shrugged his shoulders.

"Odd, yes. But not exactly his fault. Oh, yes, the police have talked to him too. Under pressure he admitted that it was Monsieur de Vigny himself who put the idea into his head—and de Vigny admits that that was so. Holland was saying something about the noise and fuss of the Carnival, and how he was all for a quiet life, and de Vigny pointed out that the solution was to work at night when St. André was noisy and sleep in the day, when it was quiet again."

The artist reluctantly abandoned this line of attack—reluctantly, for he seemed to be driven more and more to the necessity to talk to Joan Daubeney.

"And Mrs. Holland?" he hazarded, a forlorn hope promptly destroyed by Kershaw, who wearily pointed out that even if it was—naturally enough—impossible to corroborate her and her husband's story that he left her in the cottage when he went up to the court and her story that she stayed there and went to bed, yet the hard fact remained that she could not possibly have made her way into the kitchen garden without being seen.

Kershaw manifested some inclination to turn the tables and to cross-examine the artist when the latter was saved by the reappearance of Verity Brown, with Lawrence de Vigny close behind her.

"Hullo," cried Sam, as he and Kershaw rose to their feet. "All well?"

She nodded, but before she could speak Lawrence de Vigny said, in the tone of a man desperately overtired:

"I'm just going to see if Margaret's up to seeing the police yet."

He went upstairs and the others talked quietly; the conversation was mainly on the attitude of the magistrate.

"He was *ever* so polite," Verity told them. "I couldn't in the least make out what he thought about it all. His chief idea seems to be to be nice to us all, especially Lawrence."

In a very short space of time Lawrence called to them from the landing of the stairs, to the effect that his wife was prepared to be interviewed. Would they take the message . . .

"Your job," Kershaw told Samuel. "You've the gift of tongues."

So Samuel in his best French—and it is remarkable how much
better one speaks a foreign language when one is fresh than when
one is tired—successfully undertook the mission. And then, just as
the Law appeared in stately procession from the library, Joan
Daubeney, white-faced and with dark shadows under her eyes, met
them in the hall; she was arm-in-arm with her brother-in-law, who
briefly suggested that as Miss Daubeney had now come down, she
might be interviewed next. Assent was given readily enough.

"Then if you will just permit me to explain to my wife—" And
Lawrence once more ran wearily upstairs, whilst the Law proceeded as solemnly as ever to retrace its footsteps.

Samuel muttered some kind of polite yet sympathetic greeting,
which Joan acknowledged with a faint wan smile; then he and
Kershaw drew a little aside and Joan and Verity talked almost in
whispers.

Lawrence came down again; he gave Joan a smile of encouragement.

"I'll go on acting as interpreter," he said, and the pair started to
walk towards the library.

"I say, de Vigny," Kershaw checked him, "don't you think I
might go and see Burton? It's pretty clear, isn't it, that—"

"Yes," Lawrence answered, heavily yet not unreadily. "I confess that I seem to have been wrong—I don't see how he can have
done it. Anyhow, I'll put it to the police. Come along with us."

Verity and Samuel were left alone.

"Let's get out of this," she said quickly, and looked surprised
and hurt when he showed some reluctance. And his explanation
only served to puzzle her.

"I'd love to. But—I *must* talk to Joan. Just for a couple of minutes. Alone. If I stay here, I can catch her when she comes back
from the library."

"Oh, very well," said Verity stiffly, and, Kershaw at that moment reappearing, she asked him if he had obtained permission to
see Burton.

"Yes," he told her, whereupon she asked whether she might go
and see him too. "Or d'you want to talk to him—alone?" she
added.

Samuel looked at her reproachfully; but Kershaw merely said
that he was sure Burton would be delighted.

"You coming to join the deputation," he asked Samuel, "to bear
the glad tidings that Burton's to be released without a stain on his
character?"

"Mr. Horder wants to stay here," Verity said bluntly. Kershaw glanced from one to the other with a meaning twinkle.

"Dear, dear, squabbling so early?" he observed.

"Well, come along, Miss Brown. Show me the way to the prison cell, or dungeon, or whatever it is. 'Garden Room,' I think it's called."

Verity's failure even to cast him a forgiving glance as she departed effectually distracted Sam's thoughts from the problem of Louis de Vigny's death; but Joan's interrogation was a lengthy business and by degrees he banished his meditations upon feminine injustice and began to formulate the precise points which he wanted to discuss with Joan. It was idle to pretend that the scrap of paper was more than an outside chance: he had no real reason to think it had been clenched in her hand, or that she had, deliberately or accidentally, dropped it from the upper gallery. And, anyhow, what did it mean? He extracted it again from his pocketbook and stared gloomily at it. "Look at 2350." Who or what was 2350? A picture in a museum—a telephone number—a convict—or lottery ticket: these were some of his brighter ideas, rejected in turn. What in the world could there be for Joan to dash out into the garden, full of fury, to look at, round about midnight? He asked himself the question again and again—until suddenly his own phrase took on a new significance. By Jove, that might be the explanation!

If, then, the paper had been a message—possibly an anonymous one—sent to Joan? There was the incident during the bathing party; there were those voices amongst the trees; there was that key in Louis' pocket; there was Joan's angry mood when she crossed the bridge. These were the things about which—somehow—he must talk to Joan; devilish difficult, it was going to be. And . . . anyhow, he came up against that eternal blank wall: where was the weapon?

The sound of voices; Joan and Lawrence, followed by the third progress of the Law.

"Hullo, Horder? Still here? No, please don't hurry away. I—well, I thought you'd probably gone with Kershaw. Oh, Verity did, did she? Well, we're going upstairs now—to have a talk to my wife and then—why, then I think we've earned a little rest. *N'est-ce pas,* monsieur?" he turned to the magistrate and repeated his last words in French; and again a deferential assent was his reward.

"Shall I come up?" Joan spoke for the first time.

"No, my dear. You've had quite enough. Horder, will you look after Miss Daubeney? Take her out into the sunshine. It's—*triste* in here, this morning."

Joan looked at Sam, coldly, almost as if she did not see him. When they were alone, he said, nervously:

"What about it? Let's walk in the garden."

She gave a shiver.

"Garden," she repeated.

Sam thought to himself that this was carrying things too far; still, it would only make matters worse to explain elaborately that he had not intended to allude to the kitchen garden. So he contented himself with walking across and opening the door into the outer hall.

She stood motionless.

"Please," he said, with a quiet firmness which surprised himself, "I must talk to you."

Something in his tone penetrated her frozen abstraction; she looked at him with a new recognition—and was it not also with something like alarm?

"Please," he repeated, and without a word she walked listlessly through the doorway. The outer door stood open. At the threshold she looked at him inquiringly.

"Let's go through that formal garden," he suggested, "down towards the battlements that side. It's quiet there."

CHAPTER XIV

SAMUEL MAKES HAY

IN SILENCE they made their way through the bright sunlit formal garden and down to a little grassy nook where a handsome seat was set at the foot of the tall battlements. Joan Daubeney gave a little shiver and her companion hoped it was not one of repugnance; for the angle of the wall vaguely recalled that other angle in the kitchen-garden where poor Pierrot had lain in his black and white.

"Here?" she asked. "It's warm anyhow."

He was left still uncertain whether he had guessed the reason for the shiver. They sat down side by side.

"Well?" she demanded, almost fiercely.

"Miss Daubeney, you do understand, don't you, that I'm most terribly sorry—it's so awful for you—"

"Oh God," she burst out, but still angrily—to his surprise, "I was so afraid you'd start saying that. Even Margaret began—why pity *me* more than anyone else?"

"But—but—I thought—"

"Don't, then. Oh, don't you see? I liked Louis—immensely. We were such friends. But—that was all. I told him—"

"I say, I'm awfully sorry. I didn't mean to suggest—"

"I know. I'm being idiotic, but I just can't bear it . . . to be pitied, I mean, falsely. You understand what I mean? It sounds beastly of me, I suppose. It's not that I don't care. I do—terribly. But not like that. And I can't have people . . . It's—it's sort of unfair to Louis, too. Poor old Louis."

Samuel had passed through a variety of emotions at headlong speed—he had felt embarrassed, apologetic, outraged, ashamed and sympathetic. And then the girl suddenly burst into tears, and sobbed violently, and poor Sam felt both bewildered and alarmed. If she hadn't been in love with Louis—of course that might not be the truth, even if she thought it was; but if it were true, what was the matter now? No doubt the shock of it all . . .

Perhaps she read his thoughts.

"I'm sorry," she said, between sobs.

Samuel, in the best stage manner (you seldom see it on the stage) patted her on the shoulder and murmured that he was sorry too. She controlled herself by degrees, with an obvious effort, produced an inadequate handkerchief from nowhere in particular, rolled it into a ball and dabbed at her eyes with it.

"I'm sorry," she repeated. Sam felt he simply couldn't say it again, and he could think of nothing else, so this time he contented himself with another pat or two.

"Idiotic," she gulped. "But—it was so awful. So sudden. And to find him—"

"I know. Beastly.' Sam hastily interposed, rather loudly. He was in terror of another outbreak. "Still, he can't have known anything."

"No, but—" and his worst fears were confirmed.

"I say, you really mustn't, you know," he said quite firmly. "What's the use? We've got a job to do, haven't we?"

"What—what d'you mean?"

"Why, find out who—did it."

The fact that at this she sobbed even more violently, filled him with gloom, and also annoyed him.

"Did you tell the police all you knew?" he demanded, so suddenly and so abruptly that she became almost calm; she stared at him in amazement—or was it the shadow of fear which he thought he had detected before? But perhaps her earlier fear had been only that he'd start pitying her.

"Did you?" he repeated.

There was a pause. She looked away, and screwed up her handkerchief more tightly than ever.

"Why were you so angry when you ran across the upper gallery last night?"

Still no reply.

"Well, what had you got in your hand?"

This time the answer was a gasp, unmistakably of alarm and astonishment.

"What d'you mean?" she asked.

"You see," he told her. "I do know something. And you *haven't* told the police everything." He paused, quite dramatically. "Nor have I," he added.

"But—if you imagine there's anything—"

"Well, is there? I want to know, first. Miss Daubeney, it's like this. Verity and I both know that you were—well, pretty angry. We've not told anyone, and of course we don't want to, if it's got nothing to do with it. You see the police might think—"

"Think *I* killed him? You—how beastly—"

"*They* might. Of course we shouldn't. But they know nothing about you."

"Just because I was cross with him—"

"Only cross?" he asked. "I mean—please don't think I'm saying what I believe. But you must look at it from the angle the police will look at it from—if they know."

"I don't understand," she said, but Samuel did not altogether believe her.

"Well, then, if I must put it into words," he went on, rather aggrieved at what he felt to be an unnecessary task, "you had a note in your hand, hadn't you? You see, you dropped it—and I picked it up."

This time it was he who turned his eyes away; he stared straight ahead, and clenched his jaw and hoped that he looked nice and Sphinx-like. It would not do for her to detect that he was drawing a bow at a venture.

"You—picked it up. Where is it?"

"Never mind. It's safe," he said, and in spite of himself he could not keep a note of elation out of his voice. He was morally certain that Joan's eyes were full of anger as well as fear, and he was unwilling to meet them.

"Hadn't you better tell me all about it?" he suggested, still looking at the entrance to the formal garden; he failed therefore to see the little gesture of hopelessness which she made.

"Very well," she said, faintly. "There's very little to say. I saw Louis come downstairs. In an awful hurry. I called to him, but I don't think he heard. He was looking at a little scrap of paper. He looked sort of excited. Then he scrunched it up and—well, he meant to put it in the pocket of his fancy dress. But he dropped it on the floor—the stairs—instead, and didn't notice it. I was surprised—almost frightened. I don't know why. I came down after him; not all the way, just to the landing, so that I could see what he was doing."

"What did he do? Exactly?"

She wrinkled her forehead.

"Looked at the clock, I think. At any rate he stared in that direction, stock-still, and muttered something. I couldn't hear what.

Then he went—almost ran—towards the clock and took down a key. I thought it was the tennis-court key but—apparently—"

Samuel was hard put to it not to swear aloud as the girl once again broke into tears.

"You *must* pull yourself together," he told her angrily.

"S-sorry," she said, "I'll try."

"He took the key of that gate in the railings," said Sam, "though at the time you thought it was the one to the tennis-court. Well, what happened then?"

"He—he dashed off."

"And you followed him? What about the paper?"

"I—picked it up. It was all scrunched up."

"Yes, I know."

"I smoothed it out and read it."

"By the way, wasn't there a footman in the hall?"

"No, I don't think so. Very likely one walked through—every one was bustling about, you know."

"All right; now about the note."

"It—well, it didn't seem to mean anything. It just said "Look at" and then a lot of figures."

"And you had no idea what it meant?"

"No. Honestly I hadn't."

"Yet you were angry, and ran after him. Why?"

She was silent, and though he again demanded her reason, she obstinately refused to answer.

"D'you mean it was just because you thought he'd taken the tennis-court key?"

"Yes," she said, very faintly; she looked down, as if ashamed, at her hands, nervously twisting the hard-used handkerchief.

"I see." Once more Sam unconsciously sounded the note of triumph. "You were thinking of—Mrs. Holland."

If she answered this time, it was so faintly that he did not hear. Nevertheless he knew that her answer was "Yes."

"It was that bathing-party which put me on to it," (the young man's tone was painfully close to complacency), "though I hadn't thought of the key. I mean, I thought it was the note—that it was a message—"

The sound which came from his companion was more like a snort than a sob this time.

"But all the same," Sam continued, with singular tactlessness, "I don't quite see why if you didn't—I mean if you and Louis weren't, well—"

"You're perfectly loathsome," the girl burst out. "Of course it wasn't like that. I mean—oh, I suppose Louis and I were—what's the proper phrase? Indulging in a mild flirtation. And Mrs. Holland's a horrible woman, isn't she? It wasn't very pleasant to think—it was sort of insulting to me. And to Margaret too, and Verity for that matter."

"Yes, I see," Sam weakly and not too truthfully conceded.

"I'm sure you don't," was her reply, delivered with considerable spirit. "But as we're having this heart-to-heart talk—oh, you can tell the police all about it if you like—you'd better take it from me that I was certainly annoyed with Louis—just because we were friends. He was making a fool of us—and of himself, or that was what I thought. But now, perhaps I was wrong. Poor old Louis."

Alarming symptoms of recurrent lamentation impelled the young man to put another indiscreet question.

"D'you mind telling me, Miss Daubeney (I expect you've told the police but as you see the police and I don't exchange all our news); d'you mind telling me what *exactly* you saw when you went out of the Tower? Did you see it happen?"

"I've told the police," she said, and as she spoke she rose to her feet and began to walk slowly towards the Château, and Sam perforce had to walk with her. She recovered all of a sudden the frozen calm with which she had started her conversation with the artist; perhaps it was that the question brought back the atmosphere of the police inquisition for which she had deliberately steeled herself and that her nerves unconsciously repeated the duty to which she had schooled them.

"I told them," she went on, "that I just didn't see him fall. I know now that I heard the shot. Whether I did see him fall or not I don't really know. At any rate, I knew he'd just fallen. I went straight across. I think that I knew he was—dead. I suppose I screamed—twice, they say."

"Yes," said Samuel.

"I tried—you know how hard it is to find a pulse even when you're calm. Then Margaret was there and Mr. Burton, and he knelt down. The . . . the mask—And we all came in. . . . I think that's all."

"All you told the police?" asked Sam, in a low voice; they were not so far from the Château now.

"All I know—or remember," was her reply.

They walked on. Just as they reached the edge of the gravel drive—its big circular sweep in front of the main door—Sam stopped; he even made bold to check the girl by laying his hand gently on her arm.

"Where did the sound of the shot come from? Where do you think?"

She looked at him silently; she shook her arm free and moved on to the gravel.

"You can trust me," he said appealingly; his sincerity perhaps sounded in his voice. Yet she did not answer till they had reached the stone steps. He stopped at the bottom step; she went up one or two, then turned and faced him full.

"I was just at the foot of the turret stairs. The sound came from above, I'm sure."

She spoke hardly above a whisper; her expression added, "I trust you."

Sam gave a nod which was almost a bow.

CHAPTER XV

THE WORST OF THEORIES

SAMUEL FELT that his knowledge of etiquette was hardly equal to the occasion, when Joan Daubeney disappeared into the Château and left him standing on the steps. He was, after all, an outsider; Burton and Kershaw somehow seemed to be more closely involved. Obviously strangers would hardly be welcome at such a time, unless there was a cogent reason for their presence—and there was none for his. Besides which he was still feeling sore at Verity's treatment of him. Last but not least, it was high time to think of lunch. He considered every aspect of the problem and decided upon retreat. But he would not go by the shortest cut—he did not want to run the risk of encountering anyone as he went over the bridge; he would go out through the main gateway and round by the Old Town. It was a bit of a walk, certainly, but all the better if he reached the hotel after most of its inmates had finished their meal.

He slunk away down the drive and once outside the walls set out at a brisk pace. Past the railings, through which one could see the kitchen-garden, he almost ran. And then came the plunge through the soft, slippery sand of the path across the flat ground towards the road. He reached his destination crosser than ever, and bursting with heat. The *concierge* said something about the "tragic death of Monsieur Louis," but was brushed impatiently aside. The last straw was to enter the big dining-room, to find it practically deserted, but to see that its remaining occupants included the backwoods couple, looking calm and cool, and confronted by a tall green bottle of wine.

Kershaw nodded; Sam's response was very summary. But the nod was followed by a beckoning gesture, too obvious to be disregarded. Scowling, the artist turned aside from the path to his own table and approached them.

"How did you get back so soon?" he demanded.

Both the men at the table looked surprised at the question.

"Walked down by the short cut," Kershaw explained mildly. "What happened to you?"

Sam briefly explained why he had taken the longer route.

"What are the police doing?" was his next question.

"What d'you think?" Burton demanded, rather contemptuously.

"Horder means, how have they come to let you and me loose, old man," Kershaw explained with an ironical smile. Sam was too red with his pedestrian exertions for his blush to be apparent.

"No, I don't," he contradicted. "I mean, have they discovered who—did it?"

Burton shrugged his shoulders, and Kershaw shook his head.

"All they've done," said the latter, "is to satisfy themselves that none of the people who could have fired the shot, did in fact fire it. But look here, Horder, I want a word with you."

"Go on."

"The police don't want it known *how* Louis de Vigny was killed. I mean, the story is that he just suddenly took and died. See?"

"But by this time every one at St. André—"

"Oh, no, they don't. My lad, you can take it from me that at St. André when the police *and* Monsieur de Vigny say a thing, it goes."

"But what am I to—"

"You tell the same story. Honestly, you'd better. After all, we all want this cleared up, don't we?"

Rather sulkily, Sam agreed to fall in line. He was rather sceptical about the possibility of keeping the truth quiet, but if the police wanted it . . .

He went over to his own corner and set to work to do justice to the "cold table." Deliberately he failed to notice the departure of the two men, who went out on to the inevitable veranda.

In due course he, too, took his departure, but to his private balcony. What the devil was he to do now? His trip to St. André was thoroughly wrecked, but he did not want to go away. Unless Verity was going to depart—but probably she'd stay on with her two friends. And as for this afternoon . . .

A couple of cigarettes had been smoked before he decided to hire a boat and row out to explore the island. And he would take a sketch-book—and bathing clothes. Why not? How absurd to feel that it was in some obscure way disrespectful to have a swim . . . so the afternoon was passed in a tranquil solitude which was in violent contrast with the morning and night which had preceded it.

His irritation persisted; the cool sea water was soothing, but the view when he settled down to put it on paper undid all the benefit. The hotel was such a ghastly building—it seemed to dominate the whole landscape. He found a savage kind of pleasure in making it the most prominent feature of his sketch.[5]

And on top of everything when he returned to the hotel, determined to mark his superiority to Kershaw and Burton by donning a boiled shirt, he learnt that in his absence a young lady, easily recognizable from the description as Verity, had called to see him.

Undoubtedly it had been a trying day all through (needless to say, the bath was still out of order), and a simple-minded young artist might perhaps be forgiven for the frame of mind in which he stalked down to dinner.

"Pardon, monsieur, I have forgot this. The lady gave it to me." The *concierge* thrust an envelope into his hand—an ordinary hotel envelope, lavishly decorated with the name of the "Splendide" and a picture remotely resembling it. But—the note inside was signed "Verity." A radiant youth, all smiles, entered the *salle à manger,* nodded almost cordially to his acquaintances and sat down at his table to read the note again.

Verity was sorry. She had been so upset. She wanted to see him to talk about what was to be done. She was so sorry she had missed him. She thought it would be all right for her to slip down for her before-breakfast bathe. Would he be there?

Most certainly he would. And she certainly knew he would—it did not matter that he could not send an answer. He consumed coffee and brandy on the veranda; apparently the "season" had started again, for to-night, as for the Carnival, the veranda was brightly lit; his good-humour was patent to the world; his unruly sprig of hair gave him an unworldly, ingenuous look; in other words, though he went early to bed, thoroughly tired, his acquaintance had been made by nearly all the Americans in the hotel, and it was only by going to bed that he avoided knowing them all.

St. André certainly deserved to become a popular resort; that tiresome Mr. Buchan seemed to have lain no cold spells upon it, and it was singularly immune from the effect of egg-shaped depressions over Lapland and the other phenomena which make an English summer all that it ought not to be. Sam woke to find yet another gorgeous morning, and the sun shone in metaphor as well as in fact.

---

[5] See Part II. No. 5.

Verity came punctually to the shore, and she and Sam mutually forgave one another. The bathe itself was only moderately successful since the tide was low and since the girl felt that she must get back to the Château in good time. However, they managed to talk briefly, smoking their after-bathing cigarettes and sitting on the sands.

"I don't really know what to do, Sam," she said. "I mean, ought I to stay on or not? In a way, I suppose Joan's glad to have me with her, but then there's Margaret. She's terribly cut up by the awful business. I can't help feeling that perhaps the best thing is to leave the two sisters together. And then there's Lawrence. I don't know."

Sam felt that he really could not give her any advice.

"As a matter of fact," he suggested, "I don't suppose you *can* go away, can you? I mean, don't the police want us all to hang about for a bit?"

She shrugged her shoulders.

"Depends what Lawrence wants them to do, I should say. They fairly crawl to him, you know."

"Well, they rather led me to understand yesterday that I'd better be prepared for further questionings and so on, and I imagine they said the same to Burton and Kershaw. I say, by the way, what about Burton, Verity?"

"Well, what about him? Oh, I know he's a big-game hunter, and that he used to be in love with Margaret—and thinks he is still, I suppose. But—well, I talked to Joan, and she'd talked to Margaret. Mr. Burton's sentiments aren't reciprocated—and never were, if you ask me. Anyhow he seems to have come down here with the fixed idea in his head that Margaret wished she'd married him instead of Lawrence. I think he took that line the first time he talked to her alone—was it really only a day or two ago? And then at the dance he started on it again and Margaret—well, practically told him on. The *tête-à-tête* in the Tower wasn't at all what you and I thought—or feared—was it?"

Samuel agreed that if the facts were as she stated, the affair took on quite another complexion.

"Well, I must dash back and get some clothes on," Verity remarked, just regretfully enough to send the young man back elated to his hotel. Moreover, he fixed up to spend the afternoon with her, unless something unforeseen prevented it. He would look out for her by the steps up the cliff to the Château, just beyond the bridge.

He felt in no mood to talk over the case with Dandy Kershaw; he seemed to know a great deal more than he had confided to the police or anyone else, and if the truth be known he was rather afraid of the little man dragging it out of him by relentless questions. So once again he hired a boat, and spent the morning in solitude. However, as he came in to lunch, he was caught for a moment.

" 'Morning, Horder," said Kershaw. He was alone, and Sam observed that his manner suggested hurry. "Doing anything special this afternoon?"

Sam briefly explained his programme.

"I see," the other answered. "Well, that's that."

"Why? What's the idea?" Sam found himself asking.

"Oh, nothing much. I rather wondered whether you'd take charge of Burton, so to speak. You see—mind you, this is strictly between you and me—he's fed to the back teeth with St. André, and so am I too, though not for the same reason. But never mind that. The point is the police want us to hang on a few days; and Burton's down in the dumps. And Mr. de Vigny, very decently, has sent word that I'm to go and play tennis. He can't himself, of course, but there's the court and the pro. He suggests I go up this afternoon—and I'd rather like to. But Burton, of course, won't come and I don't want to leave him moping about here by himself."

Sam laughed, unfeelingly.

"That's easy," he said. "Get him buttonholed by some of the Americans who seem to be swarming in this place now."

"Harsh remedy, but not a bad idea," Kershaw agreed, smiling in turn. "Thanks for the suggestion. Don't give me away, though."

The artist promised to be wholly discreet, and went in to lunch, leaving the other in the lounge. He was highly entertained, a quarter of an hour later, to see that Kershaw had got quickly to work; he came in, the centre of a group of visitors, with Burton glowering in the rear, and carried effusiveness so far as to join the party for the meal and to compel his friend to go with him. Afterwards they all came streaming out on to the veranda, and Sam, sipping his coffee, received a blatant wink.

"What, not been to the islands?" he heard Kershaw ask. "Oh, you should. It's *the* place to see the view from." And then, a moment or two later, "I tell you what, you should get Burton to take you over. You're at a loose end this afternoon, aren't you, Billie?"

The grunt apparently was to be taken as assent.

"There you are," the little man went on boisterously. "Here's sailor and guide in one. Get a couple of boats and take a picnic tea."

"Oh, but you'll come too, Mr. Kershaw?' a girl in the party invited him, in her most ravishing manner.

"I only wish I could," he answered, with almost extravagant regret, "but I'm booked up. Now to-morrow——"

A shrill chorus began to discuss plans for the morrow; the afternoon seemed to have become a fixed and settled arrangement, though Burton manifestly was furious. Finally Kershaw got up and departed indoors, with considerable display of sorrow, and soon afterwards Samuel followed his example. As he collected his sketching outfit from his rooms, he reflected that one thing was certain, that Dandy Kershaw was an accomplished—well, call it diplomatist.

Kershaw, of course, had gone to change for his game of tennis; Sam was the first to leave the hotel. Once more he ploughed his way along that sandy path, but the prospect of finding Verity at the other end of it made the journey easy. She met him at the foot of the steps, and they plunged at once into the labyrinthine ruins of the Old Town.

"D'you really want to sketch?"

"Of course not."

"No, I don't mean that. I want to talk to you, seriously."

"Has something else happened?"

"Not exactly, but—Oh, I'll talk to you when we can find a good place to talk in."

And when they were ensconced in one of the many picturesque little courtyards, on a grassy bank below a window (which now looked as it were, from nowhere to nowhere, but which once had given the daughters of solid burghers a splendid chance to whisper to their lovers in the twilit street), Verity began:

"I can't quite make it out. Something happened this morning, but I don't know what. Margaret's up and about again now, you know. We all four had lunch together and afterwards, on the terrace, I tried to find out if they'd like me to stay or go. Well, when I asked Margaret, she and the others looked at one another in a funny sort of way."

"How d'you mean, 'funny'?"

"Oh, I can't explain. As if they knew something I didn't, or had made some arrangement on their own. Margaret and Joan kind of referred me to Lawrence, and he—well, I'd noticed at lunch that

he seemed in a funny frame of mind. Rather silent and stiff and—
yes, frightened."

"Frightened?"

"That's what I thought. Anyhow, never mind about that; he answered me, not Margaret. He said they'd been thinking things over, and talking them over, and really the best thing seemed to be for him and Margaret to go away for a bit. It wasn't settled whether Joan would go with them or not, but in any case he thought they'd leave St. André for a while. More or less shut it up, in fact."

"But they can't go away, can they? I mean, while the police—"

"That's just what I wondered. Of course, I couldn't say it bang out, like that, but I hinted—"

"Yes?" he asked, as she hesitated.

"Lawrence told me, in a very queer tone, that the police had come to the conclusion that there was no objection. Their theory was that someone—oh, in the Old Town or out in the marshes—had fired off a rifle and had shot Louis. A pure accident. Nothing else was possible."

"But, good Lord, you don't mean to say—?"

"Yes. It's *ridiculous,* isn't it? I mean it's even more impossible than—the other."

Sam nodded. The theory was obviously grotesque. How could a stray spent rifle bullet—even if it could have killed Louis—how could it possibly have entered the side of his head, when he was standing upright and in that sharp angle of the wall, too?

"What did you say, Verity?"

"What could I say? I asked Lawrence whether he agreed with the police and—he said he did. He was quite satisfied that nothing could be done."

"Then he must know who—" He stopped abruptly.

"Sam, what do you mean? No, you must tell me."

"Don't you see? You know what a pull he has with the police. If he's ready to let them get away with such an absurd theory, it must be because he doesn't want the truth to come out. In fact, I should say it's his theory, not the police's at all."

"But, my dear, why in the world would *he* want to keep it quiet? He was devoted to Louis: their occasional bickerings were just on the surface."

"I can only think of one reason," he said, in a low voice. There was a silence. She looked at him with consternation in her eyes.

"You don't mean to suggest that he himself—"

"No, that's impossible. I put that to Kershaw. There's no doubt at all that he wasn't that side of the bridge."

"Then who—"

"Well, either Joan—or Margaret."

"Joan or Margaret! You're mad, Sam. They couldn't possibly—and besides, what about the rifle? Mr. Kershaw is absolutely positive it wasn't anywhere in the Tower—"

"No, it wasn't. I'm positive of that too."

"Or in the garden. He searched it—and the police."

"Yes, that's true. That's what clears Burton."

"Then that settles it. For *I* know that neither of them had a rifle—or anything else—concealed on them." There was a silence.

"Don't you believe me?" she demanded, ready to show resentment at her entirely truthful statement being in any way questioned.

"Yes," he admitted." I do believe you. And anyhow, I don't see how concealment was possible."

"Well then," she challenged him, "how *could* it be either Joan or Margaret?"

"I don't know," he said heavily. "But otherwise, why in the name of all that's holy should Lawrence be ready to have the whole thing hushed up?"

They sat in silence.

"So I shall go back home the day after to-morrow," Verity suddenly announced.

"I—I think I will too," he told her.

"I feel I'm sort of deserting them by running away, but—"

"Let's run away together."

"Really!"

"I didn't mean that."

"Then I'm disappointed in you. However, I daresay Mother will think the more of you. She has such quaint, old-fashioned ideas. You must come and call on her."

The conversation drifted into pleasanter paths for a while.

"Hush," said Verity suddenly. "Someone's coming," and hastily she made an effort to tidy her hair and Sam lit a cigarette and moved a little farther away. The footsteps drew nearer. Sam rose to his feet and peeped through the gaping window.

CHAPTER XVI

SHUTTERS UP

AS HE PEERED OUT, the footsteps stopped; but to his surprise he could see no one. Then all of a sudden, he understood; the people—if there was more than one person—were not in the little alleyway but inside another courtyard, probably very like the one which Verity and Sam themselves had chosen, just across the alley. Indeed, he could catch a glimpse of it through an arched doorway.

Then a voice began to speak; clearly there were at least two people. And the voice sounded familiar. Sam shamelessly beckoned to Verity to listen.

"I'm very sorry," they heard, "but that's my decision—my last word."

"It's Lawrence," whispered Verity.

Sam looked surprised—it did not sound to him much like Lawrence's voice.

"He's angry," she added in explanation.

Lawrence's companion may have answered in a quiet voice; if so, the eavesdroppers missed the answer, thanks to their own whisperings.

"No, it's no use," they heard Lawrence go on (if indeed it was Lawrence). "I can't go into it all again. I'm sorry—most terribly sorry—as you know. Yes, that's true. But—nothing else is possible at present. I'm going to shut up the court, at all events for the time being. I shouldn't feel comfortable, using it. As for your husband" (the two young people positively goggled at one another), "he's under a six-months' contract. He can easily get another job and I'll help him to. People forget how many courts there are—over twenty in use in England alone, I think."

Sam found Verity at his elbow, also peeping out of the ruin of the window.

"Where?" she breathed.

Sam pointed to the archway.

"Must be Mrs. Holland," he whispered back.

She nodded; she looked as surprised as he felt.

"I'll not only do that," Lawrence went on meanwhile, "I mean, pay him in lieu of notice. But I'll make it a year's notice. And I'll keep an eye on him, you may be sure. If anything happens to him—if things go wrong—"

Sam was thrilled to see a shadow—a woman's shadow—beyond the archway; and still more to see it followed by a man's. The man seemed to be raising a minatory arm—almost as if to seize the woman's shoulder. He nudged Verity in his excitement, and with an exclamation which was anything but muffled she lost her balance—she was half kneeling on the bank—and slipped and rolled down with a clatter of stones. To make matters worse, she giggled aloud. The voices in the other courtyard fell abruptly silent. Sam, indignant at the mishap, whispered fiercely: "Talk as if we'd just come in here." She nodded, still giggling.

"Hold up, I say," he said aloud. "Are you all right?"

"Y-yes," she laughed.

"What a delightful spot," he went on; "the best we've seen."

"I don't care for it myself. Hurts too much," she answered.

"Then let's continue our exploration," said Samuel. "What's beyond this? Look out of that window."

By this time Verity was on her feet again; again she took her cue promptly and clambered up the bank again.

"Just another little street," she reported. "Oh, and it looks like another little courtyard out of it. Jolly old doorway. Let's go and see. Outside, and turn to the left."

"*En avant* then," said Sam, and together they went out by the way they had first entered.

"Pretend to have heard nothing when we meet 'em," he whispered. "Of course."

They walked round, quickly (as if in keeping with their earlier progress), to the arched doorway and into the other courtyard. They were both of them ready to be artistically astonished at meeting Lawrence and Mrs. Holland, but in fact they were genuinely astonished to see no one. A flight of steps to the left, leading up to another alley, through another doorway, obviously was the other couple's line of retreat, and no doubt it was the sound of their footsteps on those stairs which Sam had first noticed.

He looked at Verity and just in time—for her lips were framing a give-away question of the "where are they?" variety—he said:

"Not so good as the last one. But, by Jove, what a maze this place is."

"Yes, isn't it? You could get lost here as easy as anything."

"And though we haven't seen a soul all the afternoon there may be a dozen other people exploring the place all the time. No point in going through there, I think."

"You ought to come again with Margaret—she's the one who really knows her way about."

"I say, what's the time, d'you suppose? Just four o'clock." He changed the conversation with obvious intent.

"Is it really? As late as that? I ought to be getting back—why don't you come up to the Château for tea?"

"Oh, I hardly like to."

"I'm sure Lawrence would like you to. We can have it out in the garden, without disturbing anyone."

"Wouldn't that make it worse? I tell you what, you walk down to my palatial hotel. Yes, do."

She consented with some show of reluctance.

"But don't let's get involved with Mr. Kershaw—I feel I've seen enough of him lately to last me a long time."

"No fear of that," Sam assured her, and explained how the two men were spending the afternoon.

By this time they had emerged upon the path below the cliff on which the Château stood. They bore to the left, towards the bridge, and were at some pains—for fear that they might still be within earshot of Lawrence—to talk aimlessly about nothing in particular.

When they were across the bridge, Verity was full of curiosity to know why Sam had been so anxious not to let the other pair know that they had been overheard.

"It must have been Mrs. Holland," he replied—in her opinion a cryptic reply; she said as much.

"I can quite understand it, can't you?" she continued. "Lawrence wants to get rid of the taste of it all. He doesn't want a tennis professional hanging about doing nothing, while they're all away indefinitely. And he's treating them pretty well, isn't he?"

"Too well," said Sam, hastily; a further explanation was at once demanded.

He explained, feebly enough, that he merely had meant that the terms of Holland's discharge were extremely generous.

"Oh, but Lawrence is like that," she retorted. "And after all, it's hard luck on Holland, isn't it? Losing his job so very unfortunately."

The young man agreed, and again (but this time more skilfully) changed the conversation. Then he fell silent; he was assailed by a wild idea that Holland was responsible for Lawrence's departure and for his own too. A year's pay, and a promise of help to find another job, was pretty good. But how and why? Some kind of blackmail, surely. That must be it. Lawrence wants the whole business of Louis' murder hushed up—he's afraid of what may come out about Louis. And if on top of the murder, Holland turns up with some story about Louis and his wife (those "voices among the trees" kept recurring to Sam's memory), and naturally Lawrence wants to keep that quiet too? There must be an excuse for Holland to go, and to get his compensation; what more plausible way than to make it the consequence of the shutting-up of the Château? And probably Lawrence, and his wife, would be quite genuinely glad to get away for a change of scene.

Little more was said till the hotel was reached. Whilst Verity departed to tidy and powder, Sam thoughtfully ordered not only tea but also a car, to be in readiness to conduct her back to the Château afterwards.

There was no sign either of Kershaw or of Burton—so far Sam's guarantee held good. He had, however, quite forgotten how extensive an acquaintance he now possessed amongst the other visitors; their pertinacious friendliness completely ruined things. And then, before his second cup was empty, Sam caught sight of Kershaw crossing the road in front of the hotel and waving his hat as he went—not to anyone in the hotel, but—as the artist quickly realized—towards the "landing stage." That meant that both the men might be back in a few minutes.

"I say, Verity, you ought to be off," he said abruptly. Every one, Verity included, looked rather surprised; but she had by now become so accustomed to taking her cue, however sudden and unexpected, that she promptly agreed. They apologized to the four Americans who had insisted on sitting with them and fled. Sam hustled her into the car—which she condemned, very half-heartedly, as a ridiculous extravagance—and they started; Kershaw, conducting the boating party back to the hotel, caught sight of them and waved.

The car deposited Verity at the outer gate of the Château and then brought Sam back to the hotel. He slipped quietly upstairs and put in no further public appearance until dinner—incidentally he repeated his plan of coming down late, and once more it worked excellently. For Burton and Kershaw had almost finished before he began his soup.

He was not, however, destined wholly to escape. For when he in his turn was approaching the coffee stage, Kershaw reappeared from the lounge and came straight up to him.

"Sorry, Horder," he said, very gravely, "the police want you. They're out in the hall."

"Want me?" the artist repeated, startled.

"Yes, you," said Kershaw; then with a twinkling eye he added: "Don't be frightened. It's not to arrest you; on the contrary, to say you're free to come and go as you please."

Samuel hurried out into the hall, Kershaw following. A sergeant of police was there.

"*Voilà* Monsieur 'Order," said the *concierge,* and the gendarme with a flourish handed over two envelopes—one looking rather like a demand for water-rates and the other of heavy, black-edged paper. Sam opened the cheap specimen first, and with some difficulty deciphered it: the magistrate graciously announced that Monsieur Horder's presence at St. André was no longer necessary for the investigation, which was closed. He opened the other envelope, glanced at the signature and saw that it was from Lawrence de Vigny. He looked at the gendarme, who rapidly explained that officially he had only brought the official letter, but as he was coming to the hotel he had consented to bring the other also. He then requested Monsieur 'Order to sign the official envelope, in the space provided therefore, and to hand it back as his receipt. This formality complied with, he saluted and took his departure.

Kershaw touched the artist on the arm.

"Come into the lounge," he said. "There's no one there but Burton and me."

Sam hesitated, then he remembered that he had a question which he wanted to put to the little man, so he nodded.

The lounge indeed was deserted. Sam rang for a waiter, and ordered his coffee and brandy to be brought to him there.

"Er—will you have a drink or anything?" he asked the other two. Burton declined politely enough but Kershaw willingly accepted a brandy.

"And now," Kershaw began when they were finally settled, "I take it your notice is the same as mine—and Burton's. The case is over. An accident, that's all. We're free to go where and when we like."

"Yes."

"H'm. I see you feel rather the same as I do about it. But as *we* at all events leave this charming spot without a stain on our characters, I suppose there's no more for us to say."

"How d'you mean 'we'?"

"Well, we three. I shouldn't have thought the folk up at the Château—however, that's no affair of ours."

"No."

The artist's curtness brought back the twinkle to Kershaw's eye and the scowl to Burton's face.

"Burton and I mean to clear on to-morrow," the little man went on. "Back to Paris, for a start. Eh, Billie old man?"

"Billie old man" grunted, and muttered something about Africa. Kershaw made no spoken comment but flung the artist a glance of humorous resignation.

"I shall go the day after to-morrow, to London," Sam said, conscious that some pronouncement was expected of him.

"D'you mind giving me your address?" asked Kershaw. "Only just in case anything turns up."

With a rather ill-grace, he did so; in exchange he was told the Club (so to call it) at which either of the others could be "reached."

There was a pause.

Then, "What does de Vigny say?" asked Kershaw.

"Who? Oh, the letter. How d'you know—?"

"Read the signature over your shoulder. Sorry—quite an accident."

"Then I'd be glad if—"

"I know. I won't do it again. Shan't have a chance, eh?" he went on unabashed and reading Sam's thoughts accurately enough.

Sam ostentatiously pushed back his chair, and read the letter in such a way that he alone could do so.

Lawrence de Vigny expressed his very great regret at the unfortunate way in which Horder, as well as Burton and Kershaw, had been involved in the tragedy. However, the policeman who was kindly bringing the note was also bringing the official intimation that the case was at an end. He, Lawrence, though he was overwhelmed by his brother's death, was glad to feel that it had been an accident. His brother would be laid to rest in the chapel the next day; only the family and the staff would be there—he mentioned this in case any of the three men should have thought of being present. Afterwards, the Château would be shut up; he and his wife and her sister were going away and, as no doubt Horder knew, Verity was going back to London. If Sam cared to escort her—And with fresh expressions of regret and of thanks, he remained, his sincerely, Lawrence de Vigny.

Having read it through to himself, Sam cleared his throat, observed that the others might as well hear the parts with which they were still unfamiliar (this thrust was meant for Kershaw, who received it unmoved), and proceeded to read it—or most of it—aloud.

"Damned unsatisfactory," was Kershaw's comment. "Accident! Not on your life," and he advanced much the same arguments, more forcibly and convincingly expressed, as Sam had used when he discussed the theory with Verity. "I had a good look at the wound," he concluded. "It was fired from not so far away—certainly wasn't a spent bullet—and though apparently its course wasn't straight into the side of the head, but downwards, still it certainly couldn't have been a stray shot from outside the Château."

"There's just one thing I wanted to ask you," said Sam, ignoring these comments. "It's this. Suppose a rifle *was* hidden in the garden that night and we didn't find it in the darkness—could it have been taken away by one of the servants—you know, the ones we put on guard? Suppose Monsieur de Vigny had ordered them—"

"No, impossible," said Kershaw. "Oh, I know they'll do whatever he tells them, up to a point. That is, they'll hush things up. But even that is only temporary. The whole of the staff here in this hotel knows now, that Louis de Vigny was shot. Oh, yes, they do. No. I didn't tell 'em. I guess it was that old man with the balloons—yes, Pierre."

"I say, he couldn't have fired the shot, could he?"

"Of course not. Louis de Vigny was out of his sight, behind the angle of the wall. That's certain. But about the servants—well, you'll remember that *we* first asked Lawrence de Vigny to post the men out in the garden. My French is no great shakes; but I'm positive he gave no private orders about rifles—"

"No, I'm sure of that too."

"Well, let me just add this. I myself called the men in from the garden; certainly they neither of them had a rifle with 'em then. Oh, yes, the police told me it was a rifle bullet, when they told me its course in the wound. And when you're wearing knee-breeches you can't even shove a rifle down your leg. And let me just add this—that old balloon man, Pierre, was genuinely devoted to Louis de Vigny—they couldn't have handed out a rifle to an accomplice through the railings."

"But Pierre wasn't there all night?"

"The inevitable last question," was Kershaw's comment in a satisfied tone. "Answer, no, he wasn't, nor were the servants. *I* relieved them, and old Pierre was still there when I did so. And it's no use suggesting that I handed the rifle out through the railings. Because I didn't; but also—in case you don't care to take my word—I'd remind you that I could only have had one accomplice, Burton. And Burton was under lock and key all night in the library."

Burton swore at the recollection of the indignity.

"Then," said Samuel, "the police theory is as good as any other. For if you don't accept it you're driven back to this—only one of three people could have fired the shot, and none of the three had a rifle, or could have concealed it."

"That's it, in a nutshell," Kershaw answered.

"Then it's useless to discuss it any more. And if you'll excuse me I'm going to bed."

"Fine idea," was the reply. "I'll say good night and good-bye, in case we miss you in the morning. Billie, we'd better go and pack."

All three rose to their feet. Kershaw held out his hand.

"Sorry to have rubbed you up the wrong way with all my questions," he said with so frank and friendly a smile that Sam's annoyance was dispelled. He shook Kershaw's hand, and Burton's too, the latter throwing off his deep air of gloom and politely expressing a hope that one day they would meet again.

PART FOUR

THE ARCHITECT'S PLANS

CHAPTER XVII

WANTED—A DETECTIVE

IT WAS the small hours of the morning before Samuel Horder had finished his story. Henry Evelyn had kept him to dinner—the married couple made it a point of honour to produce a first-class dinner for any number of guests at the shortest notice. The two men sat on afterwards refreshing themselves with a series of whisky and sodas, and smoking endless cigarettes and pipes. The architect kept the artist's sketch-book on his knees and referred to it from time to time, as if to check the accuracy of his friend's recollection. And if from time to time he closed his eyes, it must not be thought that Morpheus interested him more than the story.

Still, it was an uncontrollable yawn which suddenly let his pipe tumble on to the hearthrug and which brought the narration to an abrupt pause.

"Sorry, old man," his host apologized.

"I'm afraid I'm boring you," the young man answered stiffly, "and, by Jove, it's fearfully late."

"Don't be a fool. I'm positively thrilled. Do go on."

"That's all."

"Oh, nonsense! What about your journey home? And where are all the rest?"

"We just came home—I didn't see either Burton or Kershaw again, as it happened."

"We? Oh, yes, you—and Miss—er—Brown."

Samuel nodded, his manner as on-hand as he could make it. Still, he blushed a little. Henry Evelyn smiled, very discreetly, of course.

"Hope you had a good crossing," he said.

"Capital."

"And may I ask—are you and Miss Brown engaged?"

"Well, no, I suppose not. I mean, we haven't—"

"I see. Well, good luck to you. I hope I'll be allowed to make her acquaintance. We shall all—"

"Of course. And you know, Henry, this is—well, you know. Different."

The older man nodded with due solemnity, and successfully disguised any inward doubt which he may have felt. He reiterated his delight and his congratulations.

"So on balance the trip was a success," he observed.

"Well, yes," was the answer. "I mean, of course, I'm frightfully pleased about Verity," he hastened to apologize for his dubiety. "But this other business—well, it's pretty ghastly. Verity, of course, feels it terribly—her best friend mixed up in it. So you see, I—"

"Yes, what exactly *do* you want?" Evelyn asked, as the other hesitated. "You said you wanted to see me, but I'm not sure why. It's very right and proper that you should come and tell me all your joys and troubles, I'm sure, but I gathered from what you said on the telephone that it was something pretty desperate."

The artist still hesitated, so his host thoughtfully provided him with another whisky. He helped himself too, and took the opportunity to drink success to his friend's designs.

"It's like this," Horder blurted out at last, taking a large gulp of whisky. "I wanted your advice. You know all sorts of people and—well, Verity and I want the business cleared up. That is, she does, and so I do too."

"You mean you want me—"

"No, no. Of course not. But I thought you'd probably know a detective. A private detective, you know. I've heard—or perhaps I read it—that you have to be jolly careful how you employ them, or they blackmail you or something."

Henry Evelyn laughed.

"Sorry. I don't know that I can help you there. I've never been mixed up in a divorce case—to my knowledge."

"Oh, I didn't mean that."

"No, I know you didn't, old man. I think I see your point. You'd like to get at the truth, but you want to be able to keep the truth quiet if it turns out to be an inconvenient one."

Horder nodded.

"And you see how things are," he said. "The murder was committed in France, and though I don't know much about French law and so on, as far as I can make out the inquiry's all over and done with. So you see—"

"I do. Mind you, I think you are rash in assuming the French police have given up. That is only what they want you to think.

However, on the one hand even if you wanted to, you couldn't bring the English police in. And on the other it's more than necessary to have a very discreet detective."

Horder again assented. Evelyn finished his drink and knocked out his pipe before he spoke again. Then he asked one or two questions which seemed irrelevant to the immediate issue.

"Is this de Vigny a French or a British subject?" was the first.

"I'm not absolutely sure. Why?" The young man was manifestly taken by surprise.

"What d'you think? And I suppose you could find out for certain?"

He thought hard for a few minutes.

"I'm practically certain he's British," he said at length. "I'm not sure whether he was naturalized or what—"

"How does he manage to keep his French title?"

"Well, he doesn't. I mean, he doesn't use it himself. But everyone there—at St. André—knows he's entitled to it—oh, by birth at any rate—and I think *they* keep it, more than he does."

"Anyhow, you could find that out for certain."

"I think so. Is it important?"

Henry Evelyn shrugged his shoulders.

"I don't suppose so. I just wondered. And now tell me something more."

"Yes?"

"What's become of the others? Mr. and Mrs. de Vigny and Miss Daubeney."

"They're still at St. André. Going off in a few days, when they've got things straightened up."

"Good. Then there's time to write and to get an answer before they go?"

"I should think so."

Nobly he refrained from another "Why?" but he so obviously wanted to ask it that the other took pity on him and provided the answer.

"It might be a good dodge to use the tennis-court as an excuse," he said. "I mean, someone might ostensibly go to play tennis but really to investigate on the spot."

"Well, but d'you think there are any private detectives who can play real tennis?"

"They'd have to learn then," Evelyn smiled. "No, but seriously, that might be a way round some of the difficulties. Suppose we sent off old Appleton, with a detective disguised as his valet, for example—"

"I say, d'you think he would?"

"I haven't the foggiest notion. Don't jump to conclusions like that. We must see. But I'll bear it in mind if necessary. You could write a note to ask if a friend of yours might use the court."

"I'm sure Lawrence de Vigny would agree. He must want it all cleared up too."

"My poor Samuel, that's the one thing which apparently he doesn't want—from what you've told me. I begin to see why your instinct told you to come to me. And now, you'll kindly note," (he spoke very emphatically), "that you're to say nothing of that suggestion to anyone—not even to your young lady—and you're not to write anything to St. André unless and until I've seen it and given my solemn approval."

Horder was not sure whether to take him seriously or not, and was a shade indignant when assured that the order was quite seriously meant. However, Evelyn insisted and rather grudgingly he agreed to obey.

"Mind you, I'm not sure that the plan will do," the older man continued. "It wants thinking about. But at first sight, the idea's attractive—old George playing away there, and making chase better than half a yard or so, and all the while his valet, pretending to lay out his clothes in the changing room and get his bath ready, is really looking for footprints and fingermarks and . . ."

Samuel laughed rudely.

"Sorry to upset your ideas," he said. "Old George will have to play by himself. Lawrence de Vigny won't be there, nor yet Holland."

"But Holland won't go yet awhile."

"Oh, he's gone by now. Apparently he and de Vigny had a proper bust-up, and he went off then and there. Verity told me. That's how we knew what Lawrence de Vigny was doing talking to Mrs. Holland."

"You forgot to tell me that you knew."

"Did I? I expect I was going to when you dropped your pipe. Anyhow, we did find out. We were a bit surprised at the time, but when Holland had the row with Lawrence de Vigny it all came out. Lawrence had been trying to break the news gently through Mrs. Holland, that was all."

"How dull," was the comment, in a dry tone. "And you got me all worked up by your account of the Couple among the Ruins."

He yawned again, largely and with no attempt at concealment, and now when the artist said it was really time he went home to his flat, he made no further effort to detain him.

"It's too late to do anything now," he said. "I think we'd better both sleep on it. Ring me up in the morning—or, I tell you what, you and Miss Brown must both come and lunch with me. Ask her in the morning, then ring me up and we'll fix details. And by then—who knows?—I may have a bright idea."

A taxi was collected, with some difficulty, and the artist departed, full of mingled thanks and apologies. Evelyn shut the front door and strolled back to the studio, to make all fast for the night and to turn out the lights. He caught sight of the artist's sketch-book lying on a low table by the fire-place, and swore amusedly at his friend's characteristic carelessness. Half idly, he sat down again in an arm-chair and took up the book and turned its pages. He liked the sketches, and thought that he would himself enjoy a trip to St. André; his head gently descended until his nose very nearly touched the pages . . .

He roused himself with a jerk, turned out the lights and, the sketch-book under his arm, clambered up the stairs to bed. But not to sleep—or not until it was nearly dawn.

Possibly he awoke when he was called, but if so it was to relapse into sleep so deep that all memory of the awakening was lost. The first thing of which he was conscious was the frantic, terrifying clamour of the telephone, which he had foolishly switched through to his bedroom over-night.

"Who? Who?" he asked in a voice husky with anger and sleepiness. "Oh, Sam. Oh yes, I remember. You came round here last night—oh, of course."

Samuel indignantly implored him to pull himself together. Had he forgotten that he'd invited Verity and him to lunch?

Evelyn apologized humbly, explaining that he had overslept himself. The artist, full of the St. André habit of early rising, snorted with contempt. By this time Evelyn's mind was clearer— clear enough, indeed, for him to wonder uneasily whether he had really thought things out after Sam had left or whether what he fancied to have been a brilliant bit of reasoning was just the fantastic child of dreams and nightmares.

As to the lunch, he expressed himself as delighted. He suggested the Berkeley at 1.15, to which Sam agreed.

"And how's Miss Brown?" Evelyn inquired.

"Oh, I think she's all right," was the answer. "I mean, I haven't actually seen her since we got back to London yesterday evening, you know. Oh, and I say, Henry, you do understand, don't you, that . . . No, never mind. I'll whisper a word in your ear before lunch. Try to be there a couple of minutes early."

Henry Evelyn was somewhat mystified. He fancied that the artist's change of mind about the question of understanding coincided with the sound of a door shutting.

"All right, Sam," he said. "By the way, are you in your flat? If so, I—"

"No, no, as a matter of fact I'm not. I met Phoebe Carstairs and her mother in Bond Street and just looked in at their house. Here she is—d'you want to speak to her?"

"Oh no," said Evelyn. "I must get up at once, or I'll be late even for lunch. Just give Phoebe my blessing."

He hung up the receiver with a quiet chuckle; how would Phoebe take the message? Then he rang for Siddons and galvanized his small household into activity, such as the preparation of hot baths, black coffee and clothes. Then there was a table to be booked for lunch and then, while the coffee was being disposed of to great advantage, there was George Appleton to be talked to.

All went well. Faithful to his promise he reached the Berkeley a minute or two before a quarter past one. He found Samuel waiting inside, evidently in an excited, not to say nervous, frame of mind.

"Hullo, Sam."

"Hullo. I say—"

"What's the secret message?"

"Steady, old man. She's here—Verity, I mean. Just behind me," (this in a sepulchral whisper). "Look here, the thing is, you won't go and talk as if Verity and I were engaged, or anything, will you? You see I don't know whether we—she—"

"Don't worry, bless you too," Evelyn assured him, and left him wondering why the slight stress had been laid on the "too."

A moment later Henry Evelyn found himself being introduced to a young lady who was singularly attractive but somehow not what he had expected. He had expected the dashing, and instead he found the demure. Not in the least Sam's type, he would have said. Perhaps she changed with her background; hadn't Sam made some allusion to an old-fashioned mother?

They went in to lunch, the host wondering whether he had not slightly overdone both the menu and the floral decorations. They talked, of course, about nothing in particular to start with and it was at this stage that Evelyn observed that Samuel's attention wandered now and again towards the far side of the restaurant. He contrived unobtrusively to follow the direction of the other's glances and detected Phoebe Carstairs lunching alone with a dark-haired youth; from what he could see of her attire at that distance and across so many obstacles, he judged that she was a radiant figure.

At length Evelyn decided to bring the conversation round to the point where he and Samuel had left it at the studio. Verity Brown, who had seemed rather bored with the proceedings up to then, displayed a prompt and lively interest. Samuel too brightened perceptibly.

"I've made up my mind," he told his guests. "You want a very special kind of detective. I'll supply your need."

"Have you found one?" asked Samuel; but Verity's expression suggested that she was tempted to put another, the right, interpretation on his words.

"No. I'm going myself," said Evelyn. Samuel gaped and Verity smiled.

"But you—of course I know—" the young man stammered.

"You've got a theory?" the girl put in.

"Perhaps. Samuel's right, of course. I'm no detective. Probably I'll make a hopeless mess of it, but even so I think I'd better have a look round before we put a professional on the job. You see, discretion is the essential. Face the facts. You may" (he addressed himself particularly to the girl) "want the whole thing hushed up—just as Monsieur de Vigny does—if the truth does come out."

She nodded. Her lip trembled, and from this and from the look in her eyes Evelyn realized more fully than he had from Sam's story how desperately anxious she was about the whole thing.

"It's—it's very good of you, Mr. Evelyn," she said.

"Mistake to thank people for good intentions," he answered lightly. "Wait till they deliver the goods. And I want your help, too. I want you to write—no, Sam had better do it—to Monsieur de Vigny to get permission for a friend of yours to play tennis in the St. André court even if the Chateau's shut up."

"Play tennis?" she echoed, questioningly.

"Yes. As I understand it, if I can get into the tennis-court, then I can get out into the kitchen-garden. The door in the Tower—Pantaloon's Tower—is fastened on the inside, isn't it? I thought so. And I imagine there's some kind of a door which closes the bridge over the river, and shuts on the Château from the outwork?"

Verity nodded again. Samuel tried to interrupt but his host went firmly on.

"Very well. That means that all we want is to have the key to the 'postern gate'—the side door to the court from the path by the cottage—left with the caretaker. Then I can use the court, so to speak, without disturbing anyone or anything."

He paused, put his hand into his pocket, and drew out an envelope.

"But look here, Henry. *You* can't play tennis. And even if you could, you can't play alone."

Evelyn half smiled, half sighed.

"Here," he said, holding out the envelope, "is a letter to Monsieur de Vigny. Put in some stuff of your own at the beginning and the end but copy this out exactly, and don't add a word to it, so far as our plans are concerned."

Samuel took it, opened the envelope and read the contents.

"But—but—Appleton. What's he to—" he began.

"Poor old George. He's agreed to give me four or five days' solid instruction here in London before we start and to continue the course at St. André."

Samuel made no attempt to conceal his bewilderment and Evelyn was not a little annoyed at his obtuseness. The artist seemed to have lost interest in the case since last night.

"So all we need now is a marker," was all he said, however. He looked at Sam, who declined to meet his eye.

"I don't quite understand," said Verity. "Do please explain."

Henry Evelyn explained. There was a silence.

The artist pursed his lips and slightly shrugged his shoulders; evidently he was not favourably impressed. Verity glanced at him with a sparkle of anger in her eyes; then she turned to Evelyn.

"I dare say I could mark—well enough," she suggested.

He smiled, and gently shook his head.

"That's very sporting of you," he said. "But—well, it would hardly do. I'm so old-fashioned, you know."

Verity did not attach undue importance to his description of himself. What interested her was the note of regret in his voice.

CHAPTER XVIII

THE WINNING OF A POINT

IT WAS A fine sunny morning at St. André. George Appleton and Henry Evelyn, who had arrived the previous evening, sat on the veranda of the Hotel Splendide and talked quietly.

"Seems a jolly nice spot," George observed, "and I'm very much obliged to you for bringing me here. I'm not sure whether it makes me a professional instead of an amateur, but never mind."

"The worst of it is," the other answered him, "I'm badly bitten by this tennis. It's the very devil—it'll ruin my orderly life. No more squash and no more lawn-tennis—and I used to enjoy 'em both once."

"If you hadn't, you'd probably have found it difficult to make as much progress as you have," he was told. "Not that you show many signs of being any earthly good."

"Pooh!" Evelyn scoffed at his seriousness. "You know quite well that already if you give me such reasonable odds as owing thirty and giving me forty and a few bisques, it's all you can do to beat me."

Appleton laughed in turn.

"Well, we'll see how we get on in the court here," he said. "When's the great match scheduled for? Fancy bringing me out here as your guest just to play tennis with me here, instead of in London."

"You forget, George. You're under my orders here. And the first one is—I'm going up alone to the court this morning. Our match is fixed for to-morrow."

As he spoke he glanced thoughtfully at the key which lay in his open palm; he had insisted on making a detour when they drove from the station to the hotel, and had made it his first duty to collect the key from the lodge.

Appleton looked at him in a puzzled way.

"I don't get the idea at all," he said. "You say you've never been here before, but you seem to know the place backwards. And what's the idea of the solitary visit to the court? No use thinking you can improve your chance of beating me by monkeying with the net or anything like that."

Henry Evelyn laughed again and rose to his feet.

"Wait and see, old son," he said, clapping his companion gently on the back. "You've got to amuse yourself this morning. I suggest a bit of a beach-crawl. Our young friend Samuel Horder found it an admirable occupation."

He made his way along the sea front and up the path to the cottage to which Sam had so often referred. The cottage was obviously shut up and untenanted; the gate which led into the garden was chained and padlocked and he climbed over it. The garden itself was trim enough, but already showed the effect of having been left unwatered during the week or so which had elapsed since the Hollands had departed. He went on his way, reached the side-door to the tennis court, unlocked it and slipped inside. The court itself distracted his attention for a minute or two from his main purpose; a feature of the game is the interest which its players inevitably take in the construction and details of the various courts still in use. Then he walked on, past the side galleries and the marker's box to the door at the far end which led, he knew, out into the miniature harbour. It was a dark corner, even by day; he found the electric-light switch but the current evidently was cut on. He opened the door, and by the light which streamed in surveyed the little workshop under the far pent-house, still littered with old racquets and the various implements needed for their repair, and so on.

Then out on to the pathway round the harbour and up into the gallery. And so stage by stage he found himself at the spots which had figured in the artist's story—as he went slowly down the turret stairs he had his first glimpse, from the narrow windows, of the corner where the body had lain.

The door of the turret was locked, and in the darkness he had some difficulty in opening it, for it was secured not only by a lock—the key was in it, on the inside—but also by two large stiff bolts. He understood how it was that Sam and Verity had heard Louis unfasten it that night. At length he stepped out into the sunshine and with a feeling of solemnity walked across the kitchen garden to the projecting angle of the wall. It was a matter only of a moment or two to satisfy himself that from the extreme point of the angle, the point where the body had lain, the walls did indeed limit the field from which the fatal shot could have been fired. He mounted the low narrow platform which followed the course of the wall—the "firing step" it would be called to-day—and looked out through the loopholes. He looked longest through one to the right—it happened, as he had gathered from Samuel's plan, to be one which gave a view of the cottage through whose garden he had walked; here was fresh confirmation of the artist's accuracy in details.

He spent some time in the kitchen garden—there was not much that he could usefully do, though he was able to satisfy himself that the doors which led from the garden up to the changing rooms and to the "gardener's cubby hole" underneath them were virtually disused. In both cases, hard as was the soil outside, it would not have been possible to open the doors without leaving the marks of heavy scrapes; once more, the artist's account was shown to be reliable.

He returned as he had come, carefully fastening behind him the door of Pantaloon's Tower. The galleries and the changing rooms were studied with no less care than the garden; a special interest perhaps was taken in the sofa where Samuel and Verity had so rapidly assumed that they were made for one another. There was nothing new to be learnt. He went down again to the tennis-court; he reflected that as his shoes were rubber-soled there was no reason why he should not inspect the court itself. Moreover, a basket of balls stood in the workshop and a racquet that had seen better days but still could hit a ball. He might as well steal a march on George Appleton by trying the pace of the court. True, the playing of tennis was only the nominal reason for his trip to St. André, but—He pursed his lips and whistled softly, as he considered the matter; he stood by the little bench, idly tapping it with a screwdriver which lay on it. Well, why not? He took up the racquet and the basket and went on to the court. A dozen or so serves made him hopeful that an underhand twist service would be effective. He crossed over to the hazard side to hit the balls back again and see how the back wall took "cut." As he approached the grille he hit a ball vigorously at it and rejoiced, as the tyro cannot fail to do, at the thud on the wooden panels—a satisfactorily hollow, booming sound. He stooped to pick up a ball, and as he did so the screw-driver which he had slipped into his pocket fell out with a clatter. He hit back towards the dedans the balls which he had served over. He propped his racquet against the corner by the grille and took off his coat. He really got busy . . .

At last he collected up the balls into the basket, put them and the racquet away where he had found them (as well as the screwdriver from his coat pocket), closed the far door, saw that all was tidy and in order, and let himself out on to the path by which he had come. Glancing at his watch he saw that he had been longer than he thought, and that George Appleton probably would be in the middle of lunch before he got back to the Splendide. George believed in regularity in the matter of meals.

His expectations were correct; his guest forgave him readily enough for his tardiness, and displayed singularly little curiosity about the way in which he had spent the morning. But he was not wholly deceived; it was part of George Appleton's philosophy to conceal his real self beneath the placid exterior of the enthusiastic athlete.

"What's the programme this afternoon?" was his only question, and he agreed quite readily to Evelyn's suggestion that they should "just take things quietly."

"I see, a training scheme," was George's comment. "The Arsenal go to Brighton, don't they, before the Cup Final?"

So the afternoon passed quietly away, till it was time for dinner, and quite soon after dinner Evelyn with another smiling reference to training proposed that it was bedtime.

"And to-morrow's the great match," said Appleton. "I'm all of a dither."

Henry Evelyn as a matter of fact did feel quite excited—rather childishly excited, he confessed to himself. He rather wished that he had not discouraged Verity Brown from coming to St. André; and even that he had tried to persuade Sam Horder to come. Drama needs an audience; George Appleton was not really suited for it—if indeed anyone could be expected to combine the parts of actor and of audience. . . .

At last the time came when the two men, racquets in hand, stepped into the court.

"I say, George," said Evelyn, as the former, having lost the spin, went to the hazard side, "I propose to change the odds. I won't have any bisques—"

"You *have* doctored the court."

"But instead it'll count a let when you hit the grille or the dedans or the winning gallery."

"What! Never heard of *that* before."

"Very likely not. But you're forever telling me to win points on the floor and not to play for winning openings. Well, let's see you do it."

Appleton grinned.

"Very well," he said. "I think you're reducing the odds, but if you like—Go ahead. Owe thirty and receive thirty—that stands?"

The game began, and it must be confessed that Henry Evelyn's performance did not suggest that he had been warranted in his reduction of the odds.

"What's the idea, Henry?" his opponent demanded when he had won the first set with surprising ease. "Your one and only idea seems to be to find the grille, and it strikes me you'll never do it."

"Just you wait, my lad, I haven't found my form yet," Evelyn grinned back.

And sure enough he made better progress in the second set, and the score reached five games all. Evelyn was serving.

"Play it out?" asked Appleton.

"No. I'll just win this game," said the other confidently, and delivered three surprisingly good serves. The fourth Appleton returned with some difficulty—his return being a high lob which bounced on the pent-house and came well out into the middle of the court. Evelyn waited for it, gripped his racquet with stern determination and smote the ball as hard as ever he could, straight into the grille.

"Good shot," was what Appleton meant to say, but the second word sounded more like "Shlord." He stared blankly at the grille. Instead of the wooden boarding, he saw a square gaping hole. Henry Evelyn dashed round from the other side of the court, catching up from one of the galleries a mysterious packet which he had brought along with him from the hotel, and tearing off the paper in which it was wrapped, to reveal an electric torch.

Appleton was still staring blankly at the grille.

"Never saw such—and what's inside—" he began.

Henry Evelyn flashed on the torch.

"We'll go exploring, George," he said. "Or, rather, Watson."

CHAPTER XIX

GAME, SETT, AND MATCH

I DON'T REALLY know much about tennis," said Verity Brown. "But I don't quite see how it happened—the grille giving way when you hit it."

She and Henry Evelyn were dining *à deux* at a quiet restaurant at the latter's urgent request on his return from St. André.

"Nor yet who killed Louis or how—in fact, I don't understand at all."

"Oh, the business of breaking the grille was a put-up job, so to speak. I just felt that the case was connected with a tennis-court and that it was proper that it should finish up with a game of tennis, even if I had to play it myself. Of course I more or less had to go over to St. André just to make sure that the solution which I'd worked out—the only possible solution, it seemed to me—was in fact the right one; but the game of tennis was just mummery. But you see the point? The case was mixed up with tennis; tennis was my excuse for going over and playing the detective; tennis was the proper way to finish it."

"I'm sorry. I'm very stupid. I still don't understand. Why not begin at the beginning? How did you reach my solution at all?"

"To be frank, I'm not sure. I mean, I hardly know whether I thought of the criminal or the method first. The method, I suppose: but it depended so much on whether Samuel's drawings were absolutely accurate. So the question of motive and so on was a kind of check."

"D'you mean the drawings which he made out there?"

"Yes. Or rather one of them. His plan showed the limits of the area from which the shot could have been fired; it seemed to be practically certain that it came from Pantaloon's Tower. From the rest of the story it seemed certain that neither Madame de Vigny nor Burton nor Miss Daubeney could have fired it."

"Yes. That was it."

"That's where Samuel's drawing of the Tower came in—the one he did from just outside the wall round the kitchen-garden. It showed the door at the foot of Pantaloon's Tower. It showed four windows above it as well as the blocked-up ones. I knew which way the spiral went; he said you stepped out to your left at the bottom of the stairs. And those things in conjunction suggested that one of the windows, the lowest but one, wasn't a window on the stairs at all."

"You mean a dummy?"

"Not necessarily—and not very likely. You can trace out the spiral for yourself; I'll show you the drawing some day. It struck me that it was quite possible the window lit a sort of hidey-hole—you know the kind of thing one calls a Priest's Hole."

The girl stared at him rather blankly.

"But how? The stairs went straight up—"

"Oh, no, they went winding up. It meant that there was a sort of double ceiling at one point, that's all. Sam and you noticed that the stairs were steeper at one point than another, or at any rate Sam noticed it—when you first took him out into the kitchen-garden. And the thickness of the walls . . . In a building that age some kind of secret passage or room seemed highly probable. Just think of the little harbour—I don't know much about smuggling in France now or in days gone by. I should be inclined to guess at what you might call political smuggling—people landing secretly, and so on."

"And the entrance was from the tennis-court?"

"That beat me at first. If there was a secret room there must be an entrance. I couldn't see where it could be—until I looked at George Appleton's rough drawing of a court. You know, I'd just thought of it as a plain rectangle like a racquet court, but the plan showed me there was at least one specially thick bit of wall—the tambour."

"But it wasn't in the tambour at all—the entrance, I mean."

"I know. And I didn't see how it could be. I just saw that there was room there for a passage in the wall. So I thought again—and the grille was so like a cupboard door that naturally one ordinarily would think it really was one. As a matter of fact the grille, I'm told, originally was a window behind which a clerk sat—the King of France thought it rather a joke to hit the clerk, I suppose, and made it a winning shot. And then as the world grew humanitarian, the clerk was allowed to put his shutters. Still, traditionally, there should be a hollow space behind the grille."

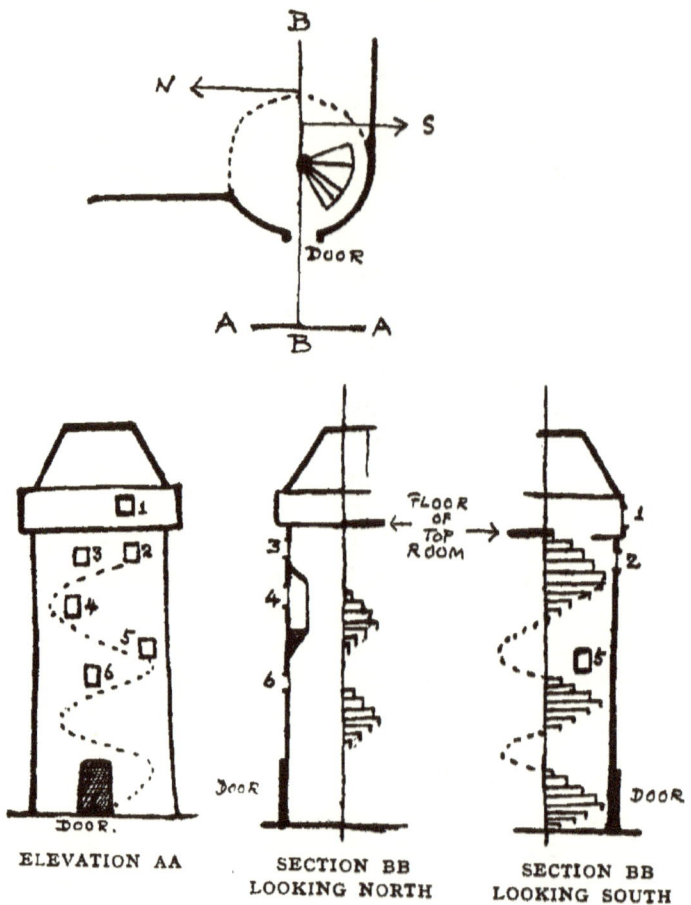

Windows 3 & 6, Blocked up; If Opened would be about
3 feet above tread of stairs.
2, about eye-height on stairs.
5, about 6 inches above tread.

Henry Evelyn's Rough Diagrams.

"Surely courts aren't all made like that? I mean, they just copy
the externals of the original—like Eton Fives Courts?"

"Oh, certainly. That remark of mine was just an aside, so to
speak. It struck me as funny that these people who played tennis
and knew so much about it didn't automatically connect the grille

with a hollow recess. Mind you, I didn't know about the original use of the grille when I started. I got on to it first because of its look and its being next door to the tambour—and so to the extra thick bit of wall. And then there was what Sam told me."

"What was that?"

"Why, how small the professional's workshop was. I just wondered whether it stopped short of the grille—and it did, just as Sam said."

"How useful it is sometimes to be an architect!"

"All the same, it wasn't altogether essential in this case. Samuel gave away the secret chamber too. Oh, certainly. As I say, he told me how the steepness of the stairs varied when he told me how he first went down them—with you. And how he brushed against the wall at one point—as if the wall was narrower just there. And on the top of that he described the scene that night in the kitchen-garden, with the light streaming out of the top window in Pantaloon's Tower—that is, the room where Madame de Vigny and Burton had been—and more light from the open door and two windows above the door. But the lights were on the staircase, weren't they? Why was there no light from the third window?"

Verity nodded energetically.

"Of course I ought to have seen that too."

"I shouldn't think any of you were in the mood to see it," he rejoined. "And I suppose an architect *is* more likely than other people to notice variety in head-room as well as in the tread, and variety in the width of the stair-well, too. Lots of people are baffled by spirals, I know."

He paused.

"Go on," she begged him. "Why did the grille collapse when you hit it?"

He smiled.

"Why, I'd seen to that the previous morning. I went up alone to the court, and left George Appleton behind. I saw that the workshop *did* stop short of the grille. So I got hold of a screw-driver, hit a ball or two about to give the court a "used" look, so to speak, and then I got busy on the grille. And I saw at once it was a solid board screwed to a framework—and the screws were pretty new. So I unscrewed them, and there was a cavity behind, and I could just see the beginning of a narrow little staircase. That was good enough. There was no desperate hurry, so I decided to play my little joke on old George. I just fixed up the grille again so that a tennis-ball propelled against it with moderate force would send it flying."

He paused again and laughed.

"I had to insist on special odds," he continued; "I didn't want to have George himself playing "Open Sesame." So I said it would be a let instead of a point to him, if he hit the grille. And then the devil of it was that *I* couldn't hit it for love or money. And when at last I did, George nearly had a fit. But he was so excited that he didn't mind ruining his flannels by coming exploring with me. It wasn't easy even to get to the little secret room itself; and there you had a tight fit when you got there. But one thing was obvious—you could fire a rifle at a man standing in the angle of the wall. And what's more—there was the rifle."

"Whose?" she asked breathlessly. "What did you do with it?"

"Left it there," he answered in a grave tone. "And I swore George to secrecy. And you're the only other person I'm proposing to tell about it. It's up to you to decide whether anyone else ought to be told."

Verity frowned. There was an interval whilst a waiter removed plates and dishes and brought others.

"Whose was the rifle?" she demanded when virtually they were alone again.

"I don't actually *know*, though I've no doubt at all in my own mind. I mean, I didn't think it wise to make inquiries—that obviously meant the police."

"Then how d'you know?"

He sighed; but his sadness was not very sincere.

"Back to the beginning," he said, "just like Snakes and Ladders."

"Who's the snake?"

"Not you."

"Then get on with the story, if you want to be forgiven for the innuendo."

"Right you are. Begin with our Samuel's first night at St. André. You remember the 'voices in the night'?"

"He told me. Louis and Mrs. Holland."

"Was it?"

"He heard her call the man Louis."

"I doubt it. Just remember, she'd an Australian accent and a habit of turning her r's into w's."

"Well? Who was it, then?"

"Wait and see, Miss Watson. Now proceed a stage further— mind you, there's probably lots of evidence you know and I don't. I have only Sam's story to go upon. According to him, there was something odd in the atmosphere at the Château—especially in the relations between the two brothers. There was the episode of the Renault car. Oh, yes, there was—or so Sam thought. Louis de Vigny hinted that his brother had deliberately done in the magneto. What was the result?"

"I haven't the foggiest idea."

"Well, Madame de Vigny was to use the other car, wasn't she? That meant that you all walked down to bathe, instead of going by car."

"Yes, well?"

"Then Lawrence wanted you—and himself, to walk down? And he was to come down after you? And I think Louis knew it— and why. What about wanting to have a word with Mrs. Holland on the way?"

"Yes, but that was Louis. Didn't Sam tell you? Louis made it very awkward all round by adding Mrs. Holland to the party. Joan was furious, and so was I, and *so* was Lawrence."

"For obvious reasons. Lawrence was annoyed because it showed that Louis knew too much, and also because it prevented him—Lawrence, I mean—from coming down a minute or two after you, or dawdling on the way, and having a word with the attractive Mrs. Holland in her rustic retreat."

"Lawrence! You mean it was Lawrence who was with Mrs. Holland the first night Sam was at St. André?"

"Obviously. Try shortening Lawrence to 'Lorrie,' and apply the "R" formula and her Australian accent."

"But no one ever called him Lorrie," she gasped.

"No one at the Château. You've no idea what he was called at the cottage."

The girl was silent, patently amazed by this new turn.

"All the trouble—as far as poor Louis de Vigny was concerned—came from that invitation to Mrs. Holland to join the bathing party," Henry Evelyn continued. "Of course, he meant well enough. He didn't approve of his brother's goings on with the woman—I expect he minded particularly because he hoped to marry Joan Daubeney. That would naturally make him anxious for Madame de Vigny's interests, wouldn't it? If she thought well of Louis, that might help him as far as Joan was concerned."

"I suppose so. But you said the cause of all the trouble—"

"So far as Louis was concerned. His brother wanted to—fix up a meeting with Mrs. Holland. That morning. He would have no other chance. He wouldn't risk a note—how could he? Servants talk. And a visit—well, Holland would be there."

"But he risked one, according to you, the night when Samuel heard the 'voices'?"

"No, I think it was by arrangement; it wasn't just luck that Holland was out—we know he was, because Sam bumped into him, at the end of the path. And besides—but I'd better go on and you'll understand better. As I see it, when Lawrence was prevented from a short private talk that morning with Mrs. Holland, she took action: she sent him a note. She had just time to tell him she'd do that, when she stopped at the garden gate to get a stone, real or otherwise, out of her shoe."

"Wasn't that just as risky?"

"She thought not. She sent it by a safe messenger."

"Who?"

"Our infant Samuel."

"What!"

"Oh, yes. You remember he carried up the parcels of the three fancy dresses she'd made. She slipped a note into the one she'd made for Lawrence. Such a brief, safe note. Just 'Look at 2350.' Or, if you like, "Look—at ten minutes to twelve.""

"Look where? What at?"

The last trace of flippancy had by now vanished from Evelyn's face; he spoke a little apprehensively—apprehensive of the effect of his words on Verity.

"The message showed in the first place that there must be some regular code, so to speak, between Lawrence and the professional's wife. He knew where to look, and what at. I expect that the figures alone would have been enough. The two words were two words too many. Poor Louis knew: I daresay he'd noticed his brother's liking for a stroll in the kitchen-garden. Oh, yes, that was where Lawrence looked *from*. And if you study Sam's map—and I've satisfied myself it's quite accurate—you'll find that from that angle in the wall, and through the loophole just to the right, you've got a clear view of the cottage. There's a gap in the trees. Just mount the 'firing step' and look out through the loophole—I suppose that if the red blind in a certain window was down it meant 'Holland is here; don't come.' And if there was no blind, but just a naked light . . . You see? So Louis was standing with the right side of his head towards Pantaloon's Tower."

"But—Louis?"

"Yes. *He* got the note, not Lawrence. Sam told me that."

"Sam *told* you?"

"Unconsciously. He told me he gave Lawrence de Vigny the parcel addressed to "L. de Vigny." But that, obviously was meant for Louis—not Lawrence. Lawrence would be 'M. de Vigny,' surely? Sam got his own parcel right. That meant that Louis put on Lawrence's dress, found the note in the pocket, and knew what it meant. 'This has got to stop,' he said to himself, and took the key of the gate in the railings and went out into the kitchen-garden. And Joan Daubeney ran after him—she'd been taken in just like you by Louis's attitude to Mrs. Holland and she'd seen him with a note—or *billet-doux,* shouldn't I call it?—in his hand. So Louis went first to the loophole, to see if the 'all clear' signal was there. We'll never know what he saw, or whether he ever got up on to the firing-step and peeped through the loophole."

Again there was an interval, whilst the waiter cleared the table and brought coffee and liqueurs.

For Verity, the interval was one of painful suspense.

"Go on," she urged at last.

"But that's all. Don't you see? Why, in those pierrot dresses you couldn't tell t'other from which of the two brothers—certainly not if you saw them some yards away, by moonlight, and you were lying cuddling a rifle, in a cramped priest's hole."

"You mean he—no, she thought—"

"*She?* No, no. Holland. Not a doubt. Lawrence hadn't managed to keep his affairs so quiet after all. We know that Louis knew—so did Holland. There's no saying how long he had known. He was one of the determined sort, who can wait, I should say. He just—waited for his opportunity. When his employer suggested that absurd hour for mending a racquet—he knew that his chance had come. He just baited the trap by telling his wife he'd be out, and busy, round about a quarter to twelve."

Verity was silent, not knowing what to say. The news, in some sort, came as a relief.

"Sam even noticed," Evelyn went on in a level voice, partly to give her time to overcome her emotion, "that the professional was dressed for the part, in grubby old clothes. I can tell you they were wanted. He must have taken a lot of the dirt away with him, and I expect he'd paid a good many visits to that secret cubby-hole. However, there was enough dust left to last me and George Appleton for a lifetime. I imagine he discovered it by chance, when he was mending the boards in the grille, and never passed on the news."

He paused for a second or two, and then resumed slowly.

"So you see why I didn't tell the police, and why it's for you to decide."

"But of course they ought to know. Oh, it's horrible to think—and Lawrence treated the Hollands so generously when he gave them notice."

"That's why. I'm pretty sure Lawrence de Vigny knows—the truth. But if the truth comes out—well, it's not a pleasant story, is it? There's his wife to consider. I should guess that he's not so attached to Mrs. Holland as to want to get her husband guillotined and marry his widow. Don't you think it's just his 'Latin' temperament? He can combine a quite sincere devotion to his wife with a *liaison* with a vulgar beauty; just like a good old melodrama."

He tried to speak lightly, but the girl still frowned, perplexed and angry and disturbed.

"It all hangs together, you see," he went on gently. "As I see it, Holland—well, let Lawrence understand that he had killed his brother. Probably he said that no one could ever prove it. Perhaps he went on to hint that he could do as much to Lawrence, and again with impunity. But equally perhaps he had his doubts. It can't be easy to feel absolutely and utterly certain that you'll get away with a murder. So his terms were not too stiff. A year's pay, help to find another job; and, of course, Mrs. Holland would be removed to a safe distance."

"You don't mean that he—that—she—?"

"That she'll be his next victim? No. I don't think you need worry: not if Sam's account of her is right. She's a sort of feminine counterpart of Lawrence de Vigny—only I should say she'll twist her husband round her little finger when she really needs to: and in future she'll know when. She's had her lesson."

Verity shivered.

"What a beastly business. How terrible for Margaret de Vigny and Joan."

"Not if they don't know."

"I see. You think they—needn't know."

"I'm sure of it. It's for you to give the word."

"Of course, it's really up to the police, isn't it?"

"No doubt. But we have our duty as law-abiding citizens, haven't we?"

"*French* police," said Verity Brown, and stared thoughtfully into her empty coffee cup. Her companion hid a smile.

"It's rather difficult for me. A responsibility," she said at length.

"I'll share it if you like," said Evelyn. "My advice is—don't tell 'em."

"That's my instinct," she agreed.

"A good combination, though I say it myself." He resumed a less serious tone. "And just to settle everything while we're about it—how much need we tell Samuel Horder, Esquire?"

"Need we tell him anything? Is he interested any longer?"

"Well, you're a better judge of that than I am."

"Oh, I'm sure I'm not."

He looked at her a little doubtfully.

"I don't mind admitting," he said, ignoring her last remark, "that I have already rung him up and told him—"

"But you said that you'd told no one—"

"Give me half a chance. I told him I'd been a complete failure as a private detective. So you can prove me a liar if you like."

"What did he say?"

"He didn't seem surprised. And now you come to mention it he didn't even sound very interested."

"I'm sure he's not," Verity remarked, rather oddly. "He's absurdly young, you know. I mean, in *mind.*"

Henry Evelyn smiled at the addition; for Verity Brown was not exactly old. She saw the smile and flushed.

"Oh, I *never* take his sort seriously," she said. "Quite amusing in a house-party, you know. But if you're trying to suggest that there's anything more in it—or that we're engaged or anything, you're right off the track. If I've got to marry at all, it'll be someone much older, who's seen a bit of the world and has got his head screwed on."

"Really?" said Henry Evelyn. "Funny you should say that. Just the opposite of me—no, not quite the opposite. If a crusted bachelor like me could ever marry—and I don't see why not—it would be someone young—young and lively and pretty, but likewise with a screwed-on head and a capacity to make up her mind."

The waiter appeared with the bill, and then departed again in search of change. Verity Brown regarded herself in a minute mirror extracted from her chain bag and smoothed her dark, shining hair. Henry Evelyn glanced casually aside and caught sight of his reflection in the mirror on the wall beside them; he too, as if unconsciously, smoothed the hair at the side of his head—there was just that "flecked with grey" effect which is—or was—so popular.

She looked up and he simultaneously turned back from the mirror. Their glances met. A smile seemed to lurk in each pair of eyes.

"Your change, sir," said the waiter.

"Change," Henry Evelyn repeated softly. "What should we do without it?" Then, more briskly, he began to discuss when Miss Brown would come to inspect the Artist's Sketch-Book, as well (he suggested) as the Architect's Studio.

THE END

RAMBLE HOUSE's

HARRY STEPHEN KEELER WEBWORK MYSTERIES

(RH) indicates the title is available ONLY in the **RAMBLE HOUSE** edition

Keeler Related Works

A To Izzard: A Harry Stephen Keeler Companion by Fender Tucker — Articles and stories about Harry, by Harry, and in his style. Included is a compleat bibliography.

Wild About Harry: Reviews of Keeler Novels — Edited by Richard Polt & Fender Tucker — 22 reviews of works by Harry Stephen Keeler from *Keeler News*. A perfect introduction to the author.

The Keeler Keyhole Collection: Annotated newsletter rants from Harry Stephen Keeler, edited by Francis M. Nevins. Over 400 pages of incredibly personal Keeleriana.

Fakealoo — Pastiches of the style of Harry Stephen Keeler by selected demented members of the HSK Society. Updated every year with the new winner.

RAMBLE HOUSE's OTHER LOONS

The Triune Man — Mindscrambling science fiction from Richard A. Lupoff
Detective Duff Unravels It — Episodic mysteries by Harvey O'Higgins
Mysterious Martin, the Master of Murder — Two versions of a strange 1912 novel by Tod Robbins about a man who writes books that can kill.
The Master of Mysteries — 1912 novel of supernatural sleuthing by Gelett Burgess
Dago Red — 22 tales of dark suspense by Bill Pronzini
The Night Remembers — A 1991 Jack Walsh mystery from Ed Gorman
Rough Cut & New, Improved Murder — Ed Gorman's first two novels
Hollywood Dreams — A novel of the Depression by Richard O'Brien
Five Gelett Burgess Novels — *The Master of Mysteries, The White Cat, Two O'Clock Courage, Ladies in Boxes, Find the Woman* with more to come
The Organ Reader — A huge compilation of just about everything published in the 1971-1972 radical bay-area newspaper, *THE ORGAN*.
A Clear Path to Cross — Sharon Knowles short mystery stories by Ed Lynskey
Old Times' Sake — Short stories by James Reasoner from Mike Shayne Magazine
Freaks and Fantasies — Eerie tales by Tod Robbins, collaborator of Tod Browning on the film FREAKS.
Five Jim Harmon Sleaze Double Novels — *Vixen Hollow/Celluloid Scandal, The Man Who Made Maniacs/Silent Siren, Ape Rape/Wanton Witch, Sex Burns Like Fire/Twist Session*, and *Sudden Lust/Passion Strip*. More doubles to come!
Marblehead: A Novel of H.P. Lovecraft — A long-lost masterpiece from Richard A. Lupoff. Published for the first time!
The Compleat Ova Hamlet — Parodies of SF authors by Richard A. Lupoff – New edition!
The Secret Adventures of Sherlock Holmes — Three Sherlockian pastiches by the Brooklyn author/publisher, Gary Lovisi.
The Universal Holmes — Richard A. Lupoff's 2007 collection of five Holmesian pastiches and a recipe for giant rat stew.
Four Joel Townsley Rogers Novels — By the author of *The Red Right Hand: Once In a Red Moon, Lady With the Dice, The Stopped Clock, Never Leave My Bed*
Two Joel Townsley Rogers Story Collections — Night of Horror and Killing Time
Twenty Norman Berrow Novels — *The Bishop's Sword, Ghost House, Don't Go Out After Dark, Claws of the Cougar, The Smokers of Hashish, The Secret Dancer, Don't Jump Mr. Boland!, The Footprints of Satan, Fingers for Ransom, The Three Tiers of Fantasy, The Spaniard's Thumb, The Eleventh Plague, Words Have Wings, One Thrilling Night, The Lady's in Danger, It Howls at Night, The Terror in the Fog, Oil Under the Window, Murder in the Melody, The Singing Room*
The N. R. De Mexico Novels — Robert Bragg presents *Marijuana Girl, Madman on a Drum, Private Chauffeur* in one volume.
Four Chelsea Quinn Yarbro Novels featuring Charlie Moon — *Ogilvie, Tallant and Moon, Music When the Sweet Voice Dies, Poisonous Fruit* and *Dead Mice*
Two Walter S. Masterman Mysteries — *The Green Toad* and *The Flying Beast*, fantastic impossible plots. More to come.
Two Hake Talbot Novels — *Rim of the Pit, The Hangman's Handyman*. Classic locked room mysteries.
Two Alexander Laing Novels — *The Motives of Nicholas Holtz* and *Dr. Scarlett*, stories of medical mayhem and intrigue from the 30s.
Four David Hume Novels — *Corpses Never Argue, Cemetery First Stop, Make Way for the Mourners, Eternity Here I Come*, and more to come.
Three Wade Wright Novels — *Echo of Fear, Death At Nostalgia Street* and *It Leads to Murder*, with more to come!
Four Rupert Penny Novels — *Policeman's Holiday, Policeman's Evidence, Lucky Policeman* and *Sealed Room Murder*, classic impossible mysteries.
Five Jack Mann Novels — Strange murder in the English countryside. *Gees' First Case, Nightmare Farm, Grey Shapes, The Ninth Life, The Glass Too Many*.
Seven Max Afford Novels — *Owl of Darkness, Death's Mannikins, Blood on His Hands, The Dead Are Blind, The Sheep and the Wolves, Sinners in Paradise* and *Two Locked Room Mysteries and a Ripping Yarn* by one of Australia's finest novelists.
Five Joseph Shallit Novels — *The Case of the Billion Dollar Body, Lady Don't Die on My Doorstep, Kiss the Killer, Yell Bloody Murder, Take Your Last Look*. One of America's best 50's authors.

The House of the Vampire — 1907 poetic thriller by George S. Viereck.

An Angel in the Street — Modern hardboiled noir by Peter Genovese.

The Devil's Mistress — Scottish gothic tale by J. W. Brodie-Innes.

The Lord of Terror — 1925 mystery with master-criminal, Fantômas.

The Lady of the Terraces — 1925 adventure by E. Charles Vivian.

My Deadly Angel — 1955 Cold War drama by John Chelton

Prose Bowl — Futuristic satire — Bill Pronzini & Barry N. Malzberg .

Satan's Den Exposed — True crime in Truth or Consequences New Mexico — Award-winning journalism by the *Desert Journal*.

The Amorous Intrigues & Adventures of Aaron Burr — by Anonymous — Hot historical action.

I Stole $16,000,000 — A true story by cracksman Herbert E. Wilson.

The Black Dark Murders — Vintage 50s college murder yarn by Milt Ozaki, writing as Robert O. Saber.

Sex Slave — Potboiler of lust in the days of Cleopatra — Dion Leclerq.

You'll Die Laughing — Bruce Elliott's 1945 novel of murder at a practical joker's English countryside manor.

The Private Journal & Diary of John H. Surratt — The memoirs of the man who conspired to assassinate President Lincoln.

Dead Man Talks Too Much — Hollywood boozer by Weed Dickenson

Red Light — History of legal prostitution in Shreveport Louisiana by Eric Brock. Includes wonderful photos of the houses and the ladies.

A Snark Selection — Lewis Carroll's *The Hunting of the Snark* with two Snarkian chapters by Harry Stephen Keeler — Illustrated by Gavin L. O'Keefe.

Ripped from the Headlines! — The Jack the Ripper story as told in the newspaper articles in the *New York* and *London Times*.

Geronimo — S. M. Barrett's 1905 autobiography of a noble American.

The White Peril in the Far East — Sidney Lewis Gulick's 1905 indictment of the West and assurance that Japan would never attack the U.S.

The Compleat Calhoon — All of Fender Tucker's works: Includes *The Totah Trilogy, Weed, Women and Song* and *Tales from the Tower,* plus a CD of all of his songs.

RAMBLE HOUSE

Fender Tucker, Prop.

www.ramblehouse.com   fender@ramblehouse.com

318-455-6847   10329 Sheephead Drive, Vancleave MS 39565

www.ingramcontent.com/pod-product-compliance
Lightning Source LLC
Chambersburg PA
CBHW030331020726
47493CB00004B/1234